PRANKENSTEIN
ON TOUR
by Andy Seed

fat fox

fatfoxbooks.com

Illustrated by Richard Morgan

PRANKENSTEIN
ON TOUR
by Andy Seed

Illustrated by Richard Morgan

For Daphne Lovdahl Papathanasiou, enjoy! AS.
To Lola. RM.

First published in 2016 by Fat Fox Books Ltd.
www.fatfoxbooks.com

ISBN: 978-1910884072

Fat Fox and associated logos are trademarks and/or
registered trademarks of Fat Fox Books Ltd.

Text copyright © Andy Seed 2016

Illustrations copyright © Richard Morgan 2016

The right of Andy Seed to be identified as the author
and Richard Morgan to be identified as the illustrator
of this work has been asserted.

A CIP catalogue record for this book is available
from the British Library.

Printed and bound by CPI Group (UK) Ltd.

Contents

1
A list of despair

Soapy Thompson held his head in his hands then let it slip and bang on the table with a hefty 'clump'.

Ouch, that was stupid. Why did I do that? he said to himself. But he knew perfectly well why he'd done it and it was because of the piece of paper in front of him. It was a list of jobs his mum had just handed him – right at the start of the school summer holidays. He should have been rejoicing that he had six weeks ahead with no maths, no spelling tests, no homework and no bullies but instead he had this.

For a start it said 'Pugh' at the top and he hated his real name. He much preferred his nickname Soapy. Everyone called him Soapy except his mum. Even his dad called him Soapy, for goodness' sake. He looked down at the list and despaired. *I bet no other kids have a list like this. It's unfair, it's wrong, it's rubbish, it smells, it stinks and it's probably some kind of crime against children.* But then again his mother was a lawyer and so she'd probably avoid that one. Still, it did stink. Lots.

PUGH SUMMER JOBS

- Tidy your room.
- Do it again properly.
- Write a thank you letter to Granny for the lace hat she sent you.
- Clean all of the hairs out of the shower plug hole.
- Scrub the patio to get rid of all those rude chalk drawings you did with your friends.
- Hoover the shed.
- Do it again properly. (I'll check).
- Play three new piano pieces.
- Learn the first 500 Chinese words in that book I gave you.
- When 1-9 are finished, come to me for the next 10 jobs.

YOU HAVE ONE WEEK

He thought back to the morning's conversation when she'd first given him the list.

"Mum, why do I have to do these things? Arvo and Loogi don't have any jobs over the summer."

She pinched her lips together. "Well, first your friends are from Estonia and so they no doubt have their own way of doing things and secondly their house is a total, well, mess."

"You're not serious about hoovering the shed, though, surely?"

"Of course I am. It gets dusty in there and I don't want any of us picking up lung infections. I spent three hours on the outside of it last week removing the potential splinters; you can remove the dust."

Soapy knew it was pointless but he carried on. "All right, but why do I have to learn 500 Chinese words?"

"Why? Why! It's the fastest growing economy on the planet, that's why. They make nearly everything we buy, they work very hard and soon they're going to be buying most of this country. If you want a job one day then you'd better learn to talk to them!"

With that she marched out.

But I don't want a job. I'm eleven. I just want to

enjoy my summer like other kids…

After three minutes, Soapy lifted his head off
the table – he'd had an idea that would cheer him
up. He picked up a blank piece of paper, grabbed
a pen and headed up to his room where he lay on
his bed and put the paper down on a Beano annual.

He smiled a crafty smile and began to write.

Mum summer jobs

- Start being fair.
- Do it again properly.
- Write a thank you letter to a chicken
  to thank it for the egg you had for breakfast.
- Collect all of your own plughole hair, make a moustache
  from it and wear it at work.
- Hoover the golf course. (All of it).
- Pretend you're a moose.
- Stop being bossy and mean.
- Play 8,359 piano pieces – with your NOSE.
- Learn 500 rude words in Chinese and write them
  on the ceiling.
- When 1-9 are finished, come to me
  for the next 10 million jobs.

Soapy was very pleased with his list and read it out loud. Unfortunately he laughed so much that he didn't hear the footsteps coming up the stairs. The bedroom door opened and Soapy's heart stopped. In a moment of madness he considered stuffing the paper into his mouth, taking a quick chew and swallowing.

It was his dad. When Soapy's father glanced down at the paper and noted the guilt written in a deep red blush across Soapy's face he raised his eyebrows.

"I would destroy that pronto if I were you," he said. Soapy nodded while slipping the paper into his hand and scrunching it hard.

Dad nearly smiled. "Right, I'm going to the golf club now and then on to the restaurant – we're fully booked tonight so I won't be back until late. I was coming up to say don't give your mother any trouble but now I know you won't because if you do I'll tell her what's on that list."

Soapy gulped then nodded again.

Dad stepped back through the door then called from the landing, "And tidy your room!"

2
The Twince wince

Soapy tore the comedy job list he'd written for Mum into tiny pieces and dropped them into the paper recycling basket she'd given him as a Christmas present two years ago. He then spent nine minutes tidying his room, which wasn't even messy, before lying down once more on his bed to read what else was on that stupid list of stupid jobs.

What? Eh?

At first, Soapy was very confused because the job list said 'Mum summer jobs' at the top when it should have said 'Pugh summer jobs'. And it was in his own handwriting.

Oh no. No no no no no no no NNNNOOOOO!

He'd torn up the wrong job list!

Soapy scrambled over to the recycling basket and tipped it onto his duvet. Out fluttered about 200 minuscule scraps of paper falling like evil confetti. He picked one up and saw a swirl of Mum's perfectly formed handwriting on it. He gave a deep groan like a panda with constipation.

Perhaps he could remember the list and write it out himself? *Right, well, there was tidying my room and er, er, writing Chinese words in the shed was it? Something about removing hairs from the piano maybe, and writing a thank you letter to the patio. No, hoover the golf course... no that was my silly list!*

He let out another panda wail and then walked over to his bookshelves and slid out the atlas, the biggest book he had, placing it on his bed. One by one he picked up the scraps of torn paper and laid them onto the atlas the right way up. Soapy then began to slide them around trying to match up the letters and reassemble his page of summer torture. It was the most depressing jigsaw in the world – and it didn't have a picture to copy.

Nearly an hour later Soapy amazed himself by carefully positioning the last torn fragment of A4 into place. He had done it and it was just about

readable. With great care he pushed himself
up from the bed and headed back to his desk
to look for some sticky tape. It was going to need
a whole roll.

Alas, in his nine minutes of tidying Soapy
had managed to put the tape somewhere other
than the drawer where he normally kept it. He
scrabbled and bumped round in boxes and bags
and for the second time that morning failed to
hear footsteps approaching. His bedroom door
swung open with the speed that only Soapy's
mum could generate and with it came a gust of
air that blew her son's hair into the sort of haircut
she would never let him have. It also blew the
reassembled scraps of ripped paper off the bed,
wafting them upwards into the
least-fun ticker tape celebration
Britain has ever known.

"Pugh, you are supposed
to be tidying your room,
not making it worse."
She almost spat.
"Get this cleared
up now!"

He had no answer.

Once the bits of paper were back in the recycling bin, Soapy reached for his phone. He tried to cheer himself up by thinking about the fact that he did actually have his own mobile when most kids his age weren't allowed one. His mum was hugely against it but Dad had given it to him as a present when he came back from some trip to the Far East or somewhere. It was only when Soapy suggested to her that it would help to keep him safe when he was out and about that Mum agreed he could keep it – she was obsessed with keeping safe.

The trouble was that although it looked like a smartphone it was actually a stupidphone. The '9' button on the keypad didn't work and the ringtone (which had once been stuck on 'clucking chicken') was now stuck on 'Justin Bieber's loudest snores'. The worst thing of all was that the predictive text didn't work and couldn't be switched off. It mangled every message he wrote, like the one he'd just sent to his best friends, Arvo and Loogi.

It should have said,

`It's the first day of the holidays and I'm already going round the bend.`

But what the phone put was,

It's the firework dance of the holdall and I'm always googling roughnecks the beard.

Luckily Arvo and Loogi were very clever and could either work out what he meant or they just gave him a call. They were identical twin brothers from Estonia who sat next to him at school and knew him very well. On this occasion they rang him, sharing the conversation by speakerphone:

"Hey Soapy, what is being up with you?" said Arvo.

"Your message was of a garble that even I, as detective of skills, could not follow," added Loogi.

Soapy was glad to hear them. "Oh, you know, it's the usual – my dad is out at golf and my mum is making my life poo. She's given me a big list of jobs to do already."

"Whotch! On the first day of the summer holiday?" said Arvo. "That is unfairness of the highest level. Have you been making of the protest?"

"There's no point. You've met my mum..."

"Yes, the meeting of her was not one of our

highlights of UK so far," said Loogi. "Perhaps we could come and assist you with this list of the tasks?"

"That's very kind but I managed to tear it up so now I don't even know what I'm supposed to do. This is already the worst summer ever."

Arvo, who liked to act as the leader of The Twince, as Soapy called the brothers, made a long 'hmmm' sound then said, "It is sounding like you are in a chutney."

"Eh?" said Soapy.

"He is meaning 'in a prickle'," said Loogi, who was usually the smarter of the two.

"In a pickle, you mean. Yes." Soapy was in no mood to laugh.

"What will you do?" said Arvo.

"I'm very tempted to do something unthinkable..."

"What?" they said together.

"To unleash Prankenstein – that would teach her a lesson."

Loogi gasped. "Surely you are not being serious?"

"Well, why not?" said Soapy. "I could just stop taking my pills then I would sleepwalk and it wouldn't be my fault if I turn into a prank-crazed monster."

"Of course it would be your fault: you are Prankenstein!" Arvo called rather too loudly.

"Sshh, fool brother," said Loogi. "Do not be telling the world. This is our big big secret, remember? Anyways, Soapy, you do not have the necessary cheese in the house because you are allergic to it. You only become the bad pranky beast if you eat the cheddar or Wensleydale or those cheese strings of the mank."

Soapy made sure his bedroom door was firmly closed. "Sure, but I could sneak next door and ask Mr Henderson if I could borrow some."

"Is the loan of cheese another of your eccentric British customs?" said Arvo. "But, whatever, it would be the biggest buffoonery of the planet World to unleash Prankenstein. Recall what he did last time…"

Loogi butted in, "For one time my brother is speaking right. Prankenstein nearly wrecked the town. He almost destroyed your house, did booby trapping of your cousin and started the war. With USA!"

Soapy chuckled. "Well, OK, he's a bit naughty but it was loads of fun. I kinda miss him."

Arvo nearly exploded. "IT WAS NOT LOADS OF FUN! He pranked us but he never gets you because you are he. Him. He."

"Okay, okay, calm down you two," said Soapy. "But I have to do something. I can't spend all summer doing boring jobs. I want to discover new pranks that I can play as a boy."

"That is sense making more," said Loogi. "Even though you never have actual done a prank."

"Well how can I in this house, with my parents?" wailed Soapy.

"Truth," said Arvo. "But worry do not, because we will come up with good plan."

"Thanks boys. I need it."

3
Win or lose?

The first day of the school summer holidays was nearly over and Soapy sat in front of Doctor Who wondering how the Twince could possibly come up with a plan to save him when he heard the sound of a car door slamming outside. This was quickly followed by the noise of a key in the front door. It was Dad, who at that moment burst into the living room, his face glowing and a dark green bottle in his hand.

"Where's your mum?" he said, almost gabbling. It was very unlike him.

"Probably in her study," said Soapy. "But why are you home now? I thought you were going to be late."

He disappeared without answering and Soapy heard him rattling around in the kitchen for glasses. Mum also heard the commotion and went into the kitchen, her brow furrowed. Soapy went to see what was going on.

"Jake? Is everything all right?" she said.

Dad came racing into the hallway holding three wine glasses. He had a dim grin across his face.

"We have something to celebrate – you're not going to believe this."

Soapy's mind raced, wondering what on earth it could be. *The lottery? Free chocolate? An escaped tiger eating the education minister who made kids do school tests all the time?*

Mum held out her hands. "Believe what?"

Dad put down the glasses and bottle on a windowsill so he could wave his arms.

"Well, you know we sell quite a lot of champagne at the restaurant to people who are celebrating birthdays and things? Well, I thought I'd try this new brand, Krogg, because they have a massive prize draw every year for companies that buy more than ten cases."

Mum raised an eyebrow. "Don't tell me you've won another sausage maker. Or a trip to World of Grapes?"

"No, just a bit better," he said, holding up a hand.

"What, Dad?" Soapy was now getting impatient.

He gave a sloppy smile. "Only a world cruise. Three weeks! For free!"

Dad opened the champagne and in his good mood allowed Soapy to have a mouthful. It was disgusting although it did produce interesting burps. Even Mum was excited about the prize and demanded that Dad give more details.

"Well, the good news is it's for a family of five so we can all go and it's round the Med, through the Suez Canal, down the Indian Ocean and right round Africa!"

"And it won't cost a penny?" said Mum.

Dad maintained his inane grin. "Totally free – all meals included and three cabins."

Soapy was bouncing on his chair. Suddenly the summer appeared a whole lot better. "Wow, when do we go?"

"Well, that's the not-so-good bit," said Dad. "It has to be in August."

"What!" shrieked

Mum, "But it's 23rd July today."

"Yes, sorry, they told me it's how it works – they fill up last minute empty spaces. Is it going to be a problem with your work?"

Soapy's mum ran a hand through her hair. "Well, Samantha can do the Watson case, and I might be able to ask Meredith to cover me for the rest. I'll have to call them tomorrow."

There was a moment's silence while they all tried not to think what would happen if Mum couldn't get off work.

"So, what's the ship like?" said Soapy.

"Woah, it's a huge liner," said Dad. *"The Queen of the Ocean,* operated by P&Q; it has eighteen decks, a cinema, seven restaurants, er, a gym, a spa and three pools – I'll show you."

He pulled a tablet computer out of a drawer

and began to tap on the screen while Soapy drew in close. Mum hesitated. "Won't the cruise be full of, er, retired people?" she said with the corners of her mouth turned down.

"Who cares?" said Dad. "Look, here it is – we get to go to Malta, Egypt, Zanzibar, Cape Town, Tenerife then back to Southampton. Come on, Fliss, you've got to admit it'll be better than yet another week in France."

"Well, I have always wanted to visit South Africa…" said Mum, nearly smiling.

After Soapy had spent a whole hour looking at photos of the ocean liner and its destinations he was sent to bed. His initial excitement had died down and he now began to think what the journey would be like.

Three weeks on a ship with my mum and dad and lots of old people. I bet there'll be no other kids. And I won't be able to go and explore 'cos Mum'll be convinced I'll fall overboard. Just the sea to stare at. I won't be able to go on bike rides or visit the shops or see my friends. It might be worse than staying here!

He tried to get to sleep but the thought of being in a small cabin with his mum and dad right next door and no chance to get away and play

with someone his own age made his brain rumble late into the night.

The following morning was Sunday and Soapy woke up late. In his mind was an idea. A fantastic idea.

The holiday is for five people... there are only three of us... I'll ask if Arvo and Loogi can come. Then it'll be fun!

The idea was totally and utterly brilliant and Soapy congratulated his brain on working away at it during the night. There was just one problem – his parents were bound to say no.

"No," said Mum.

"But it won't cost us anything and they're really nice boys and it'll stop me going doolally."

His mum, who had just found out that she could get the time off work to go on the cruise, put her breakfast coffee down and glanced upwards. "It's all right for you, Pugh. I'm sure you'll have a great time running round the ship and laughing and playing but we will be responsible for three children. One is bad enough."

Soapy turned to Dad who was pressing a huge blob of butter into his toast. "Dad, you don't mind,

do you? The Twince are really polite and sensible and they actually keep me out of trouble. If I'm on my own I'll be so bored I'll, I'll... detonate!"

Dad looked towards his wife.

"He does have a point there. Three weeks is a long time on a boat. We're happy reading and lounging but Soapy will end up pestering us. I really like Arvo and Loogi – the way they talk makes me laugh."

Good old Dad thought Soapy looking hopefully at Mum.

"Yes, granted, but we haven't even asked them – they might be going back to Estonia to see their Bazooka or whatever she's called."

"Babushka, Mum, it's their granny."

"I know, I know..."

"But they're not going. I've already texted them this morning." Mum breathed out and looked at Dad. There was a chance.

Soapy recalled the text he'd sent.

`How would you two like to come on a world cruise with me next month⌐ for free?`

His stupidphone actually put:

`Hog wound yogurt twit lies to comet on a worst crutch with my newt monkey for freezers?`

As usual the Twince called and Soapy explained about the cruise. The brothers, although excited, had a few questions:

"Is it a boat with big pointy sail?"

"Will we have to be rowing?"

"Have we opportunity chance to collect bones of wildebeest, bongo or gnu in Africa for my hobby?" (That was Arvo).

"How much of the sea puking will be forthcoming?"

Soapy had done his best to answer and then the Twince had gone to ask their parents. The boys had returned with a hoot saying they had permission.

Now Soapy was trying to listen while Mum

talked on the phone to Arvo and Loogi's dad, Olof, the sculptor of zany objects. He couldn't quite make out the words but he had the distinct impression that Mum was trying to put him off.

After fifteen of the longest minutes Soapy had ever known, Mum put down the phone, went to have a short chat with Dad then came through to the living room where their son was waiting with wide, expectant eyes.

"Well, I am completely amazed but it looks like there will be five of us on this cruise."

Soapy's whoop rattled the windows. It was just a pity he kicked over a vase in his excitement.

4
Sail of the century

The ship was hugantic, malossal, enorssive. It was as tall as an office block, as long as a traffic jam and wide as a football pitch. The three boys raced around the upper decks, exploring while Soapy's Mum and Dad read all of the safety information. The Twince had their own spacious cabin and Soapy had a small but cosy one of his own with a glass porthole looking out at the cranes of Southampton docks. His parents' cabin was really posh.

Soapy was ludicrously relieved to be on board. The previous few days had been a nightmare with his mum fussing and faffing about getting everything ready for the trip.

"You have got your anti-sleepwalking pills haven't you, Pugh? We can't have you drifting about the ship during the night or wandering overboard."

"I've told you three times I've got them already packed in my red bag."

"And you have enough for the whole trip?"

"Yes."

"And you have enough pants?"

"Yes."

"And socks?"

"Yes."

"And your own sun cream, hat, first aid bag, anti-malaria tablets, watch, spare toothbrush, comb, lip balm, ear plugs, face wipes, tweezers, floss, insect repellent, goggles, reading glasses, tissues, hankies, cotton wool, mirror, compass and whistle?"

"Yes, except I don't wear reading glasses, Mum."

"Well take some just in case – who knows what the sea will do to your eyes."

But now finally they were aboard the grand cruise liner *The Queen of the Ocean* and the hyper-fussing was all forgotten. Even Mum was impressed.

"Have you seen the ballroom? And the spa? I'm going to spend most of the three weeks in there."

Soapy and the Twince showed Dad the games room they'd discovered and then they went up to

the viewing deck to watch as the mammoth white ship pulled slowly out of the harbour and into the English Channel where it headed towards Spain and the warm Mediterranean Sea.

When they came back down they found Mum on a lower deck pointing. "What are you doing, dear?" asked Dad.

"Counting the lifeboats, just to be sure."

Soapy and the Twince enjoyed their first meal at the family buffet while their parents ate next door at the French restaurant.

"Hey, I'm being amazed that we are allowed to eat on our own like this," said Arvo.

"Yes, but you didn't hear how much my mum threatened me if we were silly."

Loogi leant in. "Also, I think we have the spy watching over us." He flicked his eyes toward a young white-jacketed steward standing by the door who was glancing their way.

"You're right," said Soapy. "My mum asked him to watch us and tell her if we looked like we were up to anything."

"Shall we be attempting to slip him the give?" said Arvo wiggling a cheeky eyebrow.

"We could give him the slip or maybe bribe him," said Soapy. "But not perhaps on the first day."

Arvo nodded. "Point good. But I think we should develop ideas for making the diversion one day so we can evade his snoopery."

"In the meantimewhile," said Loogi, "I have observed the very interesting thing. This is family buffet but where are the families? I see only two girls and one adult over far side. The rest is empty."

"You're right," said Soapy. "That place my parents are eating in was really full. Actually, I haven't seen any other kids at all apart from those posh-looking girls."

The following day the ship was right out to sea and pushing its great bulk smoothly through the dark waters as it headed south. Soapy and the Twince asked permission politely to explore the

rest of the ship. They wanted to find out if there were any more children on board.

As they toured the various decks they made whispered comments about each person they passed.

"Old."

"Very old."

"Ancient."

"Fossil."

"At least 106."

"Retired in the 1950s."

"Medical miracle."

"Zombie."

"Ghost."

"Quite young – hey!"

"That is a waiter, unwise brother."

"Oh yes, uniform is slight clue."

They sat down by one of the small swimming pools. Soapy shook his head.

"We've been everywhere now and everyone on this ship is old, except us."

"And those girls we saw buffeting yesterday,"

said Arvo.

"Wow, two posh girls and 13,000 OAPs. Great," laughed Soapy.

"If you're looking for kids there aren't any. Except us."

The three boys turned around to see two tall girls standing there. They had tanned skin and long dark hair. They were evidently twins.

"I'm Minty and this is Ursule. Hi," said the bolder girl on the left who had slightly larger eyes, but slightly shorter hair than her sister. Soapy guessed they were about twelve.

"I am Arvo and this is being my brother name of Loogi. The other kid is Soapy – he is friend, not family."

"Two sets of twins on one boat doesn't happen every day – it's cool," said Ursule who flashed a shy smile. Soapy noticed she was carrying a sketch pad.

"Are we really the only kids on this ship?" said Soapy.

Minty raised an eyebrow. "You've never been on one of these cruises before, have you?"

"Are they always the floating island of the fogey?" said Loogi.

Both girls laughed. "The way you two talk is so sweet," said Minty. "Where are you from?" "Estonia, but we are doing the living in England," said Arvo.

"We live in England too," said Minty, "but right out in the countryside. It's deadly boring. Estonia sounds really interesting."

"It is OK if you like the freezing wind, cold cabbage and strange hats," said Loogi. Again, the girls laughed. "No, I am being serious," he added with a shrug. They laughed once more.

This is really weird, thought Soapy.

"What I like about you is you're not stuck up," said Ursule. "Everyone on this ship talks about money all the time, including our parents. I love it that you boys just wear scruffy clothes and don't bother to 'dress for dinner'. It's cool."

Soapy could see that the Twince were surprised by this as they didn't consider themselves scruffy but all three boys were aware that the girls were not dressed in clothes that had come from a supermarket.

"We have to go now," said Minty, "But shall we meet tomorrow by the top pool at ten?"

The boys nodded and the girls headed towards the door giggling as they went before turning and waving.

Soapy chortled. "Something tells me those two like you."

"They are refrained girls for sure, but nice too," said Arvo. "Or am I meaning refined? Anyways, nice."

5
Shiver me timbers

Soapy was very amused the next morning when Arvo and Loogi appeared for breakfast in their smartest clothes. He asked them about it.

"Well, Minky and Herstool are girls of neatness," said Arvo.

Soapy sniggered. "It's Minty and Ursule – I think you need to get that right."

Arvo furrowed his brow. "That's what I am saying, Monty and Uzool."

"Twit brother," said Loogi. "It is Milky and Arsenal."

"Whatever," said Soapy. "But aren't we going swimming?"

"Yes, we have bathe toggings underneath," said Arvo.

The twin girls were waiting at the pool, sitting on

the side with their feet dangling in the turquoise water. They gave another giggly wave when they saw the boys.

"How is water being?" said Arvo. "Chill or cosy?"

"Oh, definitely cosy," said Minty. "Come and dip your feet in."

"Or your head," called Soapy, trying a bit too hard to make a joke.

Once the Twince had wriggled free of their woollen jackets and trousers they joined the girls at the poolside and started to kick and splash and show off a little. Soapy was determined to demonstrate how powerfully he could kick so he slammed his heels down into the water. A great explosion of droplets sprayed outwards, soaking all five children and a hefty pink-faced man lying on a sunlounger nearby.

"Oi!" he roared, sitting up and giving the kids a murderous look.

Arvo muttered, "I am thinking rapid exit advantageous here."

The others nodded, stifling nervous sniggers as they scurried away from the pool. The five of them found a quiet corner where they could talk, and Minty, the more gregarious of the girls, began to ask the boys questions.

"So, what are you three into, then?"

"Well, I am liking to collect bonce and my brother he is preferring to solve the meaty crossword puzzle."

Ursule raised her eyebrows. "You collect heads? Gosh, they have some really strange customs in Estonia."

"Not, bonce, *bonce,*" said Arvo, his brow creased.

"Yes, bonce, noggin, noodle, nut, conk – they all mean head."

Soapy stepped in, even though he was enjoying the conversation. "He collects animal bones, not heads. I prefer collecting pranks, myself."

Minty said, "Oh, you would like the stuff our mother works with: she owns a company that imports joke shop novelties."

Soapy's eyes lit up. "You have got to be kidding! You mean stink bombs, whoopee cushions and hand buzzers?"

"Exactly. When we were younger we used to enjoy testing out new things, you know, like itching

powder, blue mouth sweets and squirty flowers.
But, well, you know."

Soapy was almost bouncing. "Oh the squirting
flower is a classic but I reckon the squirting ring
fools more people. There's a pen, chewing gum
and a fake squirting cigarette too. I've got them
all. Is your mum importing any new stuff?"

"Oh, er, I've no idea, sorry."

"You could ask her, I suppose," said Ursule to
Soapy with an edge of bemusement in her voice.

While Soapy was thinking about whether this
would be a good move, Minty turned to the Twince.

"So, Loogi you are a puzzler are you? I like Sudoku myself and those code-breaking challenges."

"Ah yes," said Loogi. "The computers in the Tech Bay are having Enigma Boom. I am currently level eighteen."

"Eighteen!" screeched Minty. "I am only on five – you must be a genius."

"Hey Loogs, tell them what else you were discovering when you were online this morning," said Arvo.

Loogi nodded. "Ummm, that was being most interesting and perhaps a little shocking. I used online cruise plotter to see our sea route over next few days. After Mediterranean we go Suez Canal and then Red Sea by Egypt. Next we go Indian Ocean around Africa and it is when I am researching this I am finding great shock."

Minty and Ursule listened with wide eyes while Soapy was a bit miffed that the Twince had not mentioned this to him before.

Loogi continued, "This boat has the schedule to pass through waters near the African coast where many pirates are operating."

There was a moment's stunned silence then Soapy laughed. "What, we might be attacked by

Captain Hook or Blackbeard?"

"No, I am meaning modern sea robbers with guns and the GPS navigation," said Loogi, but no one was listening because they were too busy snorting while Soapy did impressions of Long John Silver accosting an elderly cruise passenger.

"Arrrhh, lady, give me all of your hearing aids or you'll feel the cut of me cold steel."

"Yer what? Eh? Pardon? Are you the one that does the fish fingers?"

This was followed by a long bout of pirate jokes where everyone contributed their favourite.

Why are pirates horrible?
Because they arrrrr.

Why don't pirates know their alphabet?
They think there are seven Cs.

Knock knock.
Who's there?
Interrupting pirate.
Inter– ARRRRR!

What happens if you take a pirate's pea?

He becomes irate.

Doctor, doctor, I think I'm a pirate.
I see. Open your mouth and say arrrrrr.

Once the laughter had died down Minty looked
at her watch and said that the sisters had to go.
Loogi waited until the boys were on their own and
then said, "Despite jokes of infant level it is truth
that pirates are real danger in the seas where this
liner is headed."

Soapy looked at Arvo. "We'd better keep our
cutlasses sharp then."

6
Liner diner disaster

The following Saturday evening there was an event on board the ship that Soapy really wasn't looking forward to. His mother made it clear that there was no escape, however.

"It's a formal dinner and we want you there because you have to learn how to behave on these occasions."

"But I don't like formal dinners and nor do the Twince. What is a formal dinner anyway?"

Mum pursed her lips. "Sometimes you make me want to scream. It's a meal where everyone wears smart clothes, so you need your blazer and tie."

Soapy threw up his arms. "A *tie*? But this is a holiday – you're supposed to wear flowery shorts and sunglasses and flip-flops on holiday, not suits."

"I don't think the Captain is going to be very impressed if you ruin his dinner by turning up dressed as a surfer. End of argument."

Soapy was about to say that the Twince didn't have ties or even smart shirts but his mum put up her finger in that annoying way and so that was that.

The formal dinner in the ship's main dining room was even worse than Soapy feared. All of the men wore black jackets and the women wore long dresses and kilos of showy jewellery and everyone talked in loud voices. The family had to sit at a large table with two couples they didn't know. One was a grumpy-looking woman and her even grumpier husband. The other two people were late in arriving and Soapy gulped when he saw who it was: only the hefty ham-faced man they had soaked by the pool the previous day along with a tiny lady with enormous hair. When the man saw whose table he had to share he closed his eyes and muttered something rude. The lady with him looked at the Twince with disgust, whispering into the man's ear and shaking her head. Arvo and Loogi were wearing their yellow and brown woollen jackets over hippy T-shirts. It was the best they could do.

The meal was no fun at all. Waiters fussed

around them and there were so many courses
and bits of cutlery that Soapy and the Twince
were totally confused. The hardest part was
trying to avoid the gaze of the hefty man as Soapy
pretended that he had important things to discuss
with Arvo and Loogi. Unfortunately his mum and
dad insisted on engaging in conversation with
everyone around the table. This was followed by
annoying introductions where the boys had to
pretend to smile.

It turned out that the hefty man was called
Edwin Pew.

"Ah, that's funny, our son here is called Pugh,
aren't you Soapy?" said Dad. Soapy didn't think
it was funny at all.

"Do you Pews cruise a lot?" said Mum, trying
to get more than a grunt from the hefty man.

"A couple of times a year – Caribbean, Med,
Baltic mainly."

"What about you?" said the sour-faced lady
to Mum.

"Ah, no, this is our first time. We decided it
would be very interesting to sail around Africa."

At this point Arvo surprised everyone by
joining in the conversation.

"I thought you did winning of this cruise so no choosing at all, Mrs Thompson?" She looked daggers at him.

"Er, yes, well, we did win the holiday, yes, but we still, er, had to decide to go, didn't we?"

Mr Pew looked at the Twince and Soapy and said, "Oh, you *won* it… That would explain a lot."

The conversation was driving Soapy nuts and so he did what he loved to do on these occasions and continued a silly imaginary version of the exchange in his head.

Mr P:	*How did you win it then?*
Mum:	*It was at a raffle. First prize was a dead goldfish, second was a bag of litter and third was coming on this cruise with you.*
Mr P:	*Our next trip is special. We're so wealthy that we are having The Seychelles towed to Britain so we can get there quicker.*
Mum:	*Well we're thinking about space for our next holiday. Pluto would be good or we might fly past Uranus. No, on second thoughts that's a bad idea.*

"SOAPY!"

"Er, sorry, what?"

Dad gave him a hard stare. "You've been asked three times to pass the salt. Stop daydreaming."

While he apologised again Dad asked Mr Pew what he did for a living.

"Oh, I don't need to work anymore. I made more than enough money from selling my business."

Mrs Pew then added, "Edwin was the founder of Europe's largest sick bag manufacturer."

At this point Soapy nearly choked on the bread he was eating. He tried very hard not to laugh but it wasn't enough. He swiftly covered his mouth with his napkin to stop the guffaws ringing out across the ship while Mum and Dad nodded and tried to look impressed.

Soapy glanced across at the Twince who were also amused but more controlled. He reached into his pocket and found a pen and some paper. With great sneakiness he wrote a few words out of view beneath the table.

MR PEW
Will CATCH
YOUR SPEW!

Stop the spew with Mr Pew!

He passed the message under the table to Loogi who gave a snicker then produced his own pen and scribbled something before showing an amused Arvo. The note then returned to Soapy. It said,

The only barf bags approved by Her Majesty.

Soapy did another one.

Only the best to leave your heave.

The Twince responded with,

Pew's Puke Pouches: POW!

Soon the three boys were sniggering uncontrollably and Mr Pew was clearly getting irritated by it.

"Have we missed something funny?" he said.

"N-n-no," said Soapy, putting a mammoth effort into not laughing.

The boys finally calmed down and the main

courses arrived.
Loogi had ordered
a huge red crab that
came with a set of
what looked like
metal nutcrackers.
He wasn't sure what
to do.

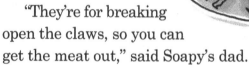

"They're for breaking
open the claws, so you can
get the meat out," said Soapy's dad.

Soapy enjoyed the next ten minutes. His own
curry was excellent but the main entertainment
was from watching Loogi wrestling with the giant
crab. He tried hitting the shell with the pliers
then crushing the edges so he could poke inside
with a knife. He forced the nutcrackers into a
gap and heaved them apart causing flecks of fishy
crustacean to fly into the air.

"Has any of it actually gone into your mouth?"
said Soapy.

Loogi had his tongue between his teeth in
concentration. "Of course. It is good. I am now going
to get into claw – waiter says it's being best bit."

He put the metal crushing tool around one

of the front legs and gave it a firm squeeze.

Nothing happened. He tried both hands and even stood up to put his weight behind the push but the crab resisted.

Arvo leant over. "You are requiring sudden force. Hit handle with shoe, maybehaps?"

Soapy thought Arvo was joking but Loogi slipped off a trainer and gave the handle a sharp whack. There was a splintering crack and bits of shell exploded in all directions. Soapy's mum made a big fuss and ordered the boys to apologise to everyone around the table but she hadn't noticed the worst thing. When the crab claw detonated, the two largest parts of the claw had gone hurtling into the air and landed on top of Mrs Pew's head. She shook the smaller one off but the larger jagged thumb of the crab was still nestled inside her extensive bouffant hairdo. Soapy and the Twince could see it sitting there like a dragon's baby in a tangled nest. Neither Mrs Pew nor any of the other adults knew it was there.

For the second time that evening Soapy found himself in pain trying not to laugh.

Finally the meal was nearly over. Soapy had

been offered cheese and biscuits but decided that, all things considered, inviting Prankenstein to the dinner was not going to be the best move.

All that remained was for everyone to toast the Captain and the voyage and then the boys could escape.

"Why are we eating toast now?" said Arvo. "Has this dinner lasted so long that it is being breakfast?"

Soapy smiled. "No, you buffoon. I know it feels that long but we aren't eating toast. We are drinking to wish the trip well."

"Toast is a drink on a ship? Now I am being total confused," said Loogi.

A steward came round and filled the adults' glasses with wine and the boys' glasses with juice. They all stood, had a slurp and it was over. Except that when Mrs Pew sat down with a jolt, the crab claw in her hair became loose and edged forward. She looked down to brush a crumb off her lap and Soapy watched with horror as the claw tumbled out of her hair and right into her glass of red wine with a plop and a splash – a splash that went right over her white silk dress. She let out a screech and Mr Pew stood up.

"RIGHT!" he roared. "That is the final straw! You brats have gone too far now!"

But Soapy and the Twince had already fled.

7
Spewy

Soapy had a lot of explaining to do when his mum and dad returned to their cabin a few minutes after the meal had ended.

"Your behaviour at that meal was a disgrace," said Mum. "Not only did you embarrass us all, you insulted Mr Pew and sprayed everyone with crab!"

Soapy held out his hands. "But it was Loogi that bashed the crab, not me, and I just got the giggles, that's all. Sick bags are funny."

"Sick bags are not funny."

Dad helped to calm things down. "I do think this is a bit of fuss about nothing. You've got to admit, dear, that Mr Pew is a bit of a grump."

"Well he may not be everyone's cup of tea but the giggling was driving him spare. And his wife's dress was ruined. And why did you rush out like that, Pugh?"

"I needed the toilet."

"It's funny how Arvo and Loogi needed the toilet at exactly the same time. Now, any more trouble from you and you're grounded."

"On a ship?"

"You know what I mean."

He did.

The following day Soapy went to find the Twince who had arranged to meet Minty and Ursule in the Tech Bay so that Loogi could show Minty how to crack the Enigma Boom game. He told them what his mum had threatened.

"It's not my fault that Spewy used to have a silly job and that it made us giggle. And it was Loogi that blasted crab into his wife's hair as well but as usual I am getting blamed for it."

Minty shook her head. "I have absolutely no idea what you are talking about."

Arvo stepped in. "The pinky-cheeked

man of bulk that we splashed at the pool a couple of days ago – he was sitting with us at the posh dinner last night."

"But who is Spewy?" said Ursule.

"Ah, that's my new nickname for him. He's called Mr Pew but he used to make sick bags so I'm calling him Spewy Pewy. Great name, eh?"

"Charming."

Then Loogi explained what happened with the crab and the wine and the five of them had a good laugh.

"It was being good thing that you did not have cheese and biscuits at end to finish everything off with bang," said Arvo, his eyes going suddenly wide as Loogi elbowed him, realising he had nearly put his foot in it and let out Soapy's big secret.

"Why would cheese and biscuits do that? Do they give you terrible wind?" asked Minty.

"No, er, I'm allergic to cheese, that's all."

Ursule still looked confused. "So why the bang? Do you swell up and pop if you eat it?"

Soapy blushed. "Something like that, yes."

"Or do you turn into the Cheese Monster?" giggled Minty.

The boys glanced at each other nervously and

there was an awkward silence.

"What?" said Ursule. "I'm sorry my sister joked about it. I know that allergies are very serious and it's probably something you're rightly worried about. I've no idea why she said Cheese Monster. Sorry."

Arvo smartly changed the subject. "Well, has anyone been seeing the pirate yet? Washpug or Blockbeard or Jock Sparrow?"

After the Foolish Five, as Minty had started to call them, had played the codebreaking game for a while they wandered out onto the deck to see if they had reached the Suez Canal which the liner was now nearing. As they leant on a railing pointing towards land a shadow blocked out the sun. It was none other than Spewy himself.

"I'm already getting sick of the sight of you kids," he said in a low growl. "I'm beginning to think that you've decided to spoil my cruise. Well, let me tell you something. If one of you comes anywhere near me or my wife again on this ship then there could just be a little accident. They can get very slippery these decks, you know. People have all sorts of falls…"

Soapy could barely believe what he was hearing. The two girls were speechless.

Loogi, however, was not. "I am not understanding in full. How can you be forecasting the accident? Accident is mishappening with no deliberate cause, yes?"

Spewy narrowed his eyes. "Are you trying to be funny, boy?"

"Humour is not my point of strength. So generally I am not attempting the wit."

The kids could see that the bulky man was thrown by Loogi's answer. "I don't like cheek or smart remarks. You wanna go first with the accident?"

Arvo tried to step in. "My brother is being portion of nut. None of us is liking the accident, the fall or the threat, so we will now leave, Mr Spew, and be giving you no more of the trouble."

Their aggressor's pink face deepened. "What did you call me?"

Soapy held up a hand and tried to push the Twince away. "He said 'Mr Pew' – it's just his Estonian accent."

"I could thump one of you right now."

As the boys edged away, they were astonished

to see Minty step forward and speak to the
snorting man. "I've no idea what makes you
think it's acceptable to threaten children half
your size but it's clear you are an exceptionally
horrible, rude and aggressive person. I would
strongly advise you to keep away from all of us
and keep your big ham-face closed."

Spewy was speechless. As the five children
backed off, Minty held up her phone. "You might
be interested to know that I recorded what you said
and will be passing it onto Soapy's mother who is

a lawyer if you give any of us any more trouble."

Spewy looked like he was going to burst with rage. The Foolish Five made their escape and once they were well out of sight and around a corner began to giggle again.

"That was speech of amazement," said Arvo.

"Well done, sis," said Ursule patting her on the back.

"Fearless and intelligent plan. Bravoo," said Loogi.

"Agreed, you're a hero," said Soapy, whose heart was still thumping. "Just one thing."

"What?" said Minty.

"Please don't tell my mum or show her your phone. She'll probably take his side."

8
Mumnap

Minty hid her phone in a safe place and despite
having the recording as evidence, the five children
kept a low profile over the next few days, avoiding
Spewy and staying out of trouble. They watched
from the top deck as the big liner passed through
the Suez Canal separating the Mediterranean Sea
from the Red Sea. There was a stopover in Egypt
where they saw the desert and met lots of flies
but, much to everyone's disappointment, spotted
no pyramids.

A few days later the ship was in the Indian
Ocean and heading down the east coast of Africa.
It was noticeably hotter on board here and for once
Soapy didn't argue with his mum about wearing a
hat. Nights were the most uncomfortable as Soapy
found that he was either too hot with covers on or
too cold with them off in his little cabin.

On the third evening in the Indian Ocean Soapy was lying awake in bed trying to get to sleep. He looked at his watch. 3.18 am. He was wondering if the Twince were also awake and what it might be like to sneak out onto the deck in the middle of the night when there was a sharp hooter sound over the ship's intercom which made him jump. Soapy's first thought was that they'd hit an iceberg but since they were sailing in tropical waters this was fairly unlikely. His next thought was that someone had set the fire alarm off but this was interrupted by an announcement.

"THIS IS YOUR CAPTAIN SPEAKING, REPEAT, THIS IS YOUR CAPTAIN SPEAKING. I HAVE AN IMPORTANT ANNOUNCEMENT. I APOLOGISE FOR WAKING YOU IN THE NIGHT BUT PLEASE LISTEN CAREFULLY. FIRST OF ALL, DO NOT PANIC. THIS IS NOT A FIRE ALARM AND THE SHIP IS NOT IN IMMEDIATE DANGER."

Soapy sat up and rubbed his eyes wondering what on earth was going on. The tinny voice continued:

"TO REPEAT, THIS IS YOUR CAPTAIN SPEAKING. PLEASE DO NOT BE ALARMED.

THE ANNOUNCEMENT IS AS FOLLOWS.
THIS VESSEL HAS BEEN BOARDED BY
A GROUP OF ARMED MEN WHO ARE
CURRENTLY ON THE BRIDGE AND HAVE
TAKEN CONTROL OF THE SHIP. EXTERNAL
COMMUNICATION SYSTEMS HAVE BEEN
SHUT DOWN AND ENGINES SLOWED.
REPEAT THIS IS YOUR CAPTAIN SPEAKING."

Soapy felt his heart race and a surge of panic
run through his body.

"DO NOT PANIC, REPEAT DO NOT PANIC.
I AM GIVING YOU THIS MESSAGE AT
GUNPOINT BUT I WILL DO EVERYTHING
NECESSARY TO ENSURE THE SAFETY OF
EVERY PASSENGER ON BOARD THIS VESSEL.
AT PRESENT, NO ONE IS IN DANGER."

Soapy thought, *Well having a gun pointed at
your head sounds quite dangerous to me.*

The announcement went on:

"THE ARMED MEN HAVE MADE THEIR
INTENTIONS CLEAR. THEY ARE DEMANDING
A TOTAL OF ONE MILLION DOLLARS IN CASH
TO BE COLLECTED BETWEEN EVERYONE
ON BOARD. THE GANG HAVE TAKEN THREE
PASSENGERS HOSTAGE, REPEAT THREE

PASSENGERS HOSTAGE. A FURTHER
ANNOUNCEMENT WILL BE MADE SHORTLY.
IN THE MEANTIME DO NOT PANIC AND
ALL PASSENGERS ARE REQUESTED TO
STAY IN THEIR CABINS."

Soapy stepped out of his cabin. The Twince
were there along with about forty other people,
all in nightwear and all looking terrified. There
was no sign of his mum or dad, however.

"Not so much of the pirate jokes now, yes?"
said Loogi, looking rather pleased.

"How can you be smiling now?" said Soapy.
"They want a million quid and I've only got £1.17
and a library card."

"Dollars is not same as Pounds, so not so bad,"
said Arvo. "Anyways,
where is your parents?"
Soapy knocked on their
door but there was no
answer.

"My mum's probably
gone in to some hyper-
naggy lawyer mode and is
threatening the hijackers
with her wagging finger,"

he said. Soapy turned the door handle and peeped into the cabin. They were not there.

Soapy and the Twince tried to find someone from the crew to see what was going on but they were told to return to their rooms by a pale and half-dressed steward.

"But my parents are missing," said Soapy. "Are you sure?" said the man.

"Come and see for yourself."

At this point a door opened along the corridor and Soapy's dad bustled through with another steward. He was still in his dressing gown. He rushed up to Soapy.

"Don't worry, son, but your mum's been kidnapped by desperate armed pirates."

For once, Soapy didn't know what to say. He wondered if the pirates knew what they were letting themselves in for. Dad carried on, hugging Soapy as he spoke.

"I went to the loo and when I came out she wasn't there. I checked to see if she'd gone onto the deck for some fresh air and that's when I saw these guys with guns running about and shouting."

Soapy gulped. Even though his mum was strict

and the world's biggest fusser, he'd prefer her not to be forced to walk the plank. "Where is she now?"

"On the bridge with the Captain, senior officers and the other two hostages – a member of the crew Security Team just told me. I have to stay here though and look after you three."

"Who are the other hostages?" said Soapy. "It's that Pew bloke and his wife, they said."

Soapy, Dad and the Twince sat in his parents' large cabin and waited for something to happen. Soapy felt strangely calm but his dad was jiggling about, scratching his neck and muttering constantly. He stood up and paced about, thinking hard. The Twince meanwhile talked to each other in low whispers, no doubt hatching some potty plan using Loogi's problem-solving capabilities. Soapy checked his phone.

"There's still no signal. These hijackers must really know what they are doing with all the tech stuff."

"I told you previous," said Loogi. "Twenty-first century pirate has digital hacking skills and fiendy plans, not ho-yo-yo and pieces of nine."

"Nor skull and cross bonce," added Arvo, who

was twiddling with a toad tibia as he often did when thinking.

Dad wasn't even listening but now launched into an epic moan. "Oh, why did this have to happen to us? Couldn't they have kidnapped one of those rich grannies and just taken her pearls or something? Your mum is going to be SO cross. I'd hate to be those hijackers now... But anyway, this should never have happened – the liner should be protected against these pirates. Our holiday is ruined – I am going to demand our money back."

"We never paid for the cruise, though, Dad," said Soapy.

"That's beside the point. I want my wife back and I want some kind of really good compensation."

"I am not liking to raise the nasty question but, what will happen if kidnappers do not get the one million dollars?" said Arvo.

"I've already asked that but the crew won't tell me," said Dad.

At this point, there was a loud knock and the cabin door swung open. In stepped one of the ship's security officers along with a female steward who tried to smile at the boys.

The man cleared his throat. "Er, right, Mr Thompson, there is some news. The hijackers have clarified their position and things are happening quickly."

"OK, well?" said Dad, his eyebrows up to the ceiling.

"Well, they say that the million dollars needs to be given to them in the next thirty-five minutes because after that naval or coastguard boats will start to arrive."

"But what about my mum?" said Soapy.

"Ah, yes, well, the pirates say that if the money is not received in that time the hostages will be cut adrift at sea in a plastic raft with no food. They will have to eat each other."

After this there was a short, desperate period of silence. *Well at least Spewy could keep Mum going for a few months.*

Dad came out of his shock. "Well, have you collected the money? Have you asked the passengers to cough up?"

The steward now spoke. "Yes sir, we rushed around everyone with collecting bags immediately."

"And?"

"We raised $439.16, sir. A bit short of a million, I'm afraid."

Loogi nodded, "$999,560.84 to be precisely."

Dad threw up his arms. "But this cruise is full of wealthy people!"

"Erm, they said they didn't have any cash. Some said they'd never heard of your mother and didn't know if she represented value for money... sorry."

"What are we going to do?" said Soapy.

The security man tried to sound positive. "Well, do you have any money, sir?"

Dad went to his wallet. "Only a few pounds. Do pirates accept credit cards?"

"I don't think so, sir."

"How about UOI?" said Arvo. "No, I am meaning IOU."

"What about the crew – there are hundreds of them? Don't they have money?"

The steward hung her head. "We did get some money off them, and the head chef offered his best spatula but it's against the cruise operator's policy, I'm afraid. Sorry."

Dad was now turning purple. "Well it's against my policy to let my wife be fed to sharks by a bunch of sea-robbers! There must be SOMETHING we can do."

9

Rescue plandemonium

The security officer raised a finger. "We do have a sort of plan, Mr Thompson."

"What is it?" said Dad sounding very doubtful.

"Right, well, you come with us to the bridge and speak to the kidnappers. You can explain that this is your wife they have as hostage and that your children are on board too. Are all three boys here yours?"

"No, just one."

"Well, maybe tell them it's three. Or seven, and a dribbling baby perhaps."

"But why?"

"Well, according to my Happy Hijack Handbook 1986, if you can arouse some sympathy in the hijackers they might at least lower their demands."

"I would have to have a family the size of India for them to come down to 439 dollars... but I suppose it's worth a try. What about the boys here?"

"They'll be fine. Steward Burns here will look after them."

Dad looked at Soapy and the Twince. "OK, but be good you three, all right? Don't hatch any silly rescue plans."

The security man opened the door and Dad stepped out with him, wearing his tough negotiating face. The steward remained behind and closed the door.

Soapy went to the far side of the room, sat on the bed and beckoned the Twince over. He put his head forward and said in a whisper, "Right, who has a good rescue plan?"

After a brief mumbled discussion where the

three boys all agreed that the security officer's idea would never work there was a quiet tap at the door. The steward opened it and there were Minty and Ursule, both in their pyjamas.

"Yes?" said Steward Burns.

Minty answered with a solemn face. "We're friends of the boys here and have come to give them support while they're going through this awful crisis. Also, we have wine gums."

"Our parents said it's OK," added Ursule.

The steward looked doubtful but she agreed it couldn't do any harm and so she let them in.

Minty offered her a black wine gum as reward, which helped seal the deal.

The twins shuffled over to the bed and joined the huddle of plotters.

"The Foolish Five are back together and we'll come up with some really good rescue plans," whispered Minty.

"We're sorry about your mum," added Ursule, kindly. "I'm sure she'll put up a fight, though."

Soapy groaned. "That's part of the problem – she's probably given them such a telling off that they've already thrown her in the sea."

"Time is doing the running out," said Arvo. "We are needing ideas quick."

"Agreed," whispered Soapy, "But keep your voice down so that the steward can't hear."

There then followed a brainstorm of possible

ideas.

We sneak out, pinch some of the posh passengers'
jewellery and give that to the pirates.
Bang out an SOS signal on the side of the
ship using Arvo's bones.
Find out how to turn the lights out then
jump on them in the dark.
Give them the pile of cash and while they're
counting it, grab their guns.
Use mobile phone torches to signal to some
kind of elite rescue squad.
Throw crabs at them.

All five knew that none of these plans was going to
work and that most of them were completely daft.

"One big problem is that we are in this cabin
with a steward blocking the door," said Soapy. "We
need to get out if we are to do something to help."

"I have an idea," said Ursule. "I could pretend to
go to the loo and call that I am in difficulty in there."

Loogi looked confused. "What, you mean you
have fallen down toilet?"

"Giant poo stuck, is possible?" added Arvo.

"I was meaning more that I didn't feel well."

"Oh, right," said Soapy who was thinking along the same lines as the Twince.

Ursule carried on. "I call her and she comes over then I dash out and we lock her in the loo and escape to rescue your mother."

"Good plan, sis, but isn't the lock on the inside?"

"Yes, but we could shove the bed against the door," said Soapy.

"This bed is being fixed to floor and wall," said Arvo.

"Everything is fixed down on a ship," said Minty. "It's so things don't slide about in a storm."

Ursule nodded. "OK, so we can't lock her in but it will give us all a moment to run out of the door and escape this cabin. We can run faster than her, I'm sure."

Everyone agreed that was a good idea.

"If only we had a plan to actually rescue my mum," wailed Soapy quietly.

"Well, there is being one way…" said Loogi.

"What?" whispered Minty, suddenly sounding excited.

"We do the sneak to the kitchens and give Soapy cheese."

"What!" screeched Soapy, causing the steward

to look their way.

"Oh, you mean so that he explodes and causes a diversion so the pirates can be overpowered?" said Minty. "It's a bit drastic, isn't it? Losing a son to get a mother back?"

"It's certainly drastic," said Soapy, "But it is our only hope."

"What exactly do you mean?" said Ursule, curiously. "What really happens when you eat cheese?"

Loogi held up a hand. "I am sorry most deep – we cannot be telling you that."

10
Prankenstein on board

Minty and Ursule asked lots of questions but Soapy and the Twince refused to divulge the truth about Prankenstein.

"I'm sorry, it's secret and if word ever got out then... anything could happen. It will be so bad that the world could end. Or worse," said Soapy.

"Wow, whatever could it be?" said Minty. "Anyway, you're clearly not going to tell us and time is running out for your mum so you'd better go and do whatever shocking thing it is and hope it works. Ursule and I will distract the steward with the toilet plan then we'll stay here while you three go off. Ready?"

The boys nodded and Ursule got up holding her stomach and pulling a queasy face. The steward noticed. She went into the loo, closed the door and started coughing and spluttering. The boys heard the taps running, the toilet being flushed and lots of groaning followed by a faint cry of, "H… h… help…"

Minty stood up. "Are you all right, sis?" She looked at Steward Burns. "I think she's not well."

The steward went over and knocked on the door asking if Ursule was OK while inside louder wails and thumps could be heard.

The steward turned the handle and went inside. Minty nodded to the boys and, as stealthy as hunting cats, they stole over to the cabin door, turned the handle and slipped out.

The corridor outside was gloomy, lit by a small lamp, but much to the boys' relief it was now clear of people. They began to move towards the exit that would take them to one of the staircases and down to the ship's galleys.

"I am thinking we should go back way," said Arvo. "Security peoples will be patrolling main staircases."

"Good idea," said Soapy. "Let's go to the back of the boat by the games room where that small stairway is."

"What are we actual doing?" said Loogi as they crept along. "I know you are unleashing Prankenstein, Soapy. But you are not doing the sleepwalking. Is that mattering?"

Soapy stopped. "I don't know, I hope not. I just need to eat some cheese and find out.

Prankenstein is the only person who can stop these hijackers and save my mum."

After a slow and chilling journey where they were twice nearly spotted by stewards and where they heard one of the pirates shouting orders in an unknown language, the three boys reached one of the ship's kitchens. Soapy found a large refrigerator and inside was what they were looking for: cheese.

"Double Gloucester," he said, picking up a large plastic-wrapped piece. "One of my deadly enemies."

"If you are eating this, you know what is going to be happening?" said Arvo.

"Yes, well, no," said Soapy.

Loogi put his fingers against his cheeks. "This is problem. If you turn into Prankenstein then anything can be happening, *anything!*"

Arvo nodded. "The bad beastie may rescue your mum and trick pirates but likely he will also be pranking others much – like us. He has done it before. Many will suffer…"

Soapy held out a hand. "But what else can I do? It's my mum's only hope. She may be bossy, mean and a safety-mad spoilsport but she is my mum. I've got to try and help her. Sorry boys."

He looked for a knife to cut a piece of cheese.

"It is big risk, he is out of control, but we agree," said Loogi.

Soapy broke off a chunk of Double Gloucester and stared at it, as if it were deadly poison. Arvo gulped. "Shall we stay and watch? We have never seen transformation before."

Soapy nodded. "It's up to you. Here goes…"

11
Pirate prank-fest

The following day was one of the strangest in the lives of every person on board *The Queen of the Ocean,* not least the eight heavily-armed pirates who had hijacked the giant cruise liner and thought they were in charge. Nobody could really explain what had happened in the last part of the night.

The ship's light had gone out at 4.06am and everything was plunged into blackness. There were screams and shouts, bumps and bangs, a few small explosions, several torch beams waving around and lots of people, saying 'oof' as they banged their heads or stubbed a toe trying to escape.

At 4.47am as the first light of dawn was beginning to gather on the eastern horizon, the ship's lights came back on and everyone was amazed. Lots of things had happened. The captain soon made another announcement to say that the ship was once more under the control of the crew and the Royal Navy was on its way. There was cheering and whooping everywhere.

Minty and Ursule were allowed to leave the Thompsons' cabin and go and see their parents.

After that they ran to find the Twince who were sitting on their beds looking spectacularly groggy. "Isn't it great news?" called Minty. "Soapy did it! Well, I presume it was him."

"Where is he?" said Arvo. "Is he being back in his cabin?"

"We don't know," said Ursule. "We thought you'd know."

The four of them went along to Soapy's door and knocked. There was no answer. They peered inside and found his bed empty.

"Is he with his mum and dad, maybe?" said Minty.

The Thompsons' cabin was empty too.

"Wherever could he be?" said Ursule. "He's the hero of the hour."

Loogi looked at his brother and shrugged. "He could be being anywhere. This is bad, very bad."

Minty was just about to ask why it was so

bad and to add that he was probably just with his parents when the corridor exit door burst open and Mr and Mrs Thompson came through surrounded by a gaggle of fussing stewards and security people.

Mum pushed them away. "Just let me breathe and do stop talking. I just need a cup of coffee. Well, four or five – very strong cappucinos. And I need to lie down. Hello boys. Where is Pugh?"

The Twince tried to answer but Dad bundled Mum into the cabin and told everyone else to go away before closing the door. Three seconds later, he opened it and told the Twince to come in.

"Isn't Soapy with you, boys?" said Dad. "My wife's a bit worried." They saw Mrs Thompson swallow some headache pills then roll around on the bed gurgling.

Arvo answered, "Er, no, we are not knowing where he is. We were thinking he was with you."

"Maybe he's just gone to the toilet or something?" said Dad. He then spent five minutes looking for his wife's mobile phone so she could call her family and tell them she was OK. As the two of them searched, Arvo and Loogi stood there wondering what on earth Soapy, or rather

Prankenstein, was up to at that precise moment. And where was he? They thought back to a few hours previously when they had watched their friend eat a lump of cheese.

The effect had been instantaneous. Soapy had begun to shake and bounce, his hands and feet and neck swelling as if he were being inflated by a steam pump. His eyes had bulged horribly and he let out a stupendous series of trumps, burps and noises that the Twince had never heard before. They had shrunk back, alarmed but unable to stop watching.

The next stage was a change of colour. Soapy went red then greeny-brown while ugly lumps began to sprout across his face and limbs. He continued to jolt and bump, growing broader and more solid as big muscles erupted all over him. His feet were now steaming and his face became contorted and impish with large pointed ears and yellow eyes. Big black hairs were now emerging all over his skin. He was no longer Soapy.

The Twince had fled in terror and as they ran they heard a piercing howl.

The phone was finally found and as Mum made

her calls Dad once more asked the Twince where Soapy might be.

"He was with you when I left here. Did he go out somewhere?"

Loogi nodded, "Er, yes, Mr T, he went to be looking for food."

"Oh, hungry again... well, that doesn't surprise me. He's probably in the breakfast buffet. I'll go and find him."

"But what happened with the pirates?" asked Arvo. "We are not knowing and the captain gave no information on the announcing."

Dad's eyes lit up. "You don't know? Oh, I suppose not... well, it's truly amazing and quite a mystery. The cruise operators must have some kind of awesome stealth Ninja team on board because those hijackers were well and truly dealt with. Either that or the SAS arrived and no one saw them in the dark."

Loogi was now jiggling in his desperation to know the outcome. "Are the kidnappers being dead?"

"Dead?" laughed Dad. "No, they're now captured and they're going to be brought to justice. My wife's already lined up sixty-five separate charges. Anyway, this is what happened: she was on the bridge one moment with the captain and senior officers, all being held at gunpoint by these three masked men and then the lights went out. She says there was lots of bumping and groaning and shouting and then it went quiet. The First Officer switched on a torch and, astonishingly the hijackers were gone. The door was open, their guns were on the floor and no one had a clue what had happened."

Arvo and Loogi glanced at each other while Dad carried on.

"But that wasn't even the strangest thing that happened in the scuffle. When the torch was shone around to see if everyone was OK, the Captain had an Elvis wig glued to his head, the Communications Officer's trousers were gone and, er…" At this point he glanced at his wife who was talking down her mobile at 300mph. "Er, my wife was standing in a large bowl of chicken soup."

The Twince looked over at Mrs Thompson's feet and could see that they were wet, with small pieces of broccoli stuck between her toes. Mr Thompson was very surprised that the boys were not surprised.

"Were Mr and Mrs Spew, er, Pew, pranked also?" asked Loogi.

"No, my wife said they weren't being held there with her, which is odd."

"What was became of the hijackers?" said Arvo.

"Well, it was hard to see anything in the dark but when the lights came back on they were all found in the main upper deck pool, eight of them."

"What, they were having swim?" gasped Loogi.

"No, they were in a lifeboat in the middle of the pool. Somehow there were three sharks in the pool too and the boat was full of large nipping crabs and lobsters. Those guys were not happy."

"Er, wow," said Arvo.

"Yes, double wow," said Loogi.

Dad scratched his head. It's all a total mystery and none of the crew seems to know who did this – or they're not willing to tell maybe – but it's completely incredible that it all happened in about half an hour."

The Twince were about to ask more questions when they heard Soapy's mum end her call.

"Right," she said, "Thank heavens that is over. Now, I need a shower and more coffee. And where is our son?"

12
The big secret

Mrs Thompson went to have a shower, Mr Thompson went to look for Soapy in the breakfast buffet room and the Twince returned to their cabin. Arvo twiddled some bat bones in an agitated manner while Loogi chewed hard on his crossword pen.

"We now have big problem," said Arvo. "Soapy is missing, Prankenstein is on loose and this ship could be destroyed by his extreme pranking."

Loogi furrowed his brow. "Let us not be leaping to the conclusion, hasty brother. It is now morning and on all other occasions Prankenstein has turned back into Soapy at this time. Maybe he is just sleeping somewhere on the boat?"

"But he is not in his bed. That is bad sign. He could be anywhere."

"And did something strike you as odd-strange

when Mr T told us the events of the night with the hijackers?"

"Yes, in the deed it did. What happened to Mr Spew and crabby wife?"

"Correct. They too were taken as the hostage along with Soapy's mum but they were not on the bridge with the Captain and gunmen. I am wondering why…"

"Maybe they were held as the hostage in other place on board?"

"But why? Anyways, let us hope that Prankenstein pranked them huge time!"

At that moment the ship's intercom gave another 'bing-bong' sound and the captain made a further announcement.

"I AM PLEASED TO REPORT THAT THIS VESSEL IS NOW COMPLETELY SECURE. ALL OF THE PIRATE HIJACKERS HAVE NOW BEEN ROUNDED UP AND PLACED UNDER ARREST. THEY ARE CONFINED IN A SECURE AREA AND WILL BE DEALT WITH BY ROYAL NAVY PERSONNEL WHO ARE DUE TO REACH OUR CRUISE LINER IN

APPROXIMATELY FOUR HOURS. ALL THREE HOSTAGES ARE SAFE AND WELL AS ARE THE MEMBERS OF THE CREW WHO WERE HELD AT GUNPOINT. THERE WILL BE A FULL INVESTIGATION INTO THE EVENTS OF THE LAST ELEVEN HOURS.

WE HOPE THAT LIFE ON BOARD THE LINER CAN RETURN TO NORMAL AND THAT YOU CAN CONTINUE TO ENJOY YOUR CRUISE AS BEFORE. A ROYAL NAVY PATROL BOAT WILL ESCORT US THROUGH THESE WATERS UNTIL WE REACH OUR NEXT PORT. FINALLY, I HAVE A REQUEST TO MAKE FROM THE SHIP'S HEAD CHEF. IF ANYONE HAS SEEN A 4KG PIECE OF ROQUEFORT CHEESE THAT HAS GONE MISSING FROM THE SHIP'S MAIN GALLEY WOULD THEY PLEASE INFORM A MEMBER OF STAFF AS IT IS NEEDED FOR HIS FAVOURITE RECIPE. THANK YOU."

Arvo and Loogi looked at each other in silence. Each was biting a lip. A familiar sense of doom filled their cabin.

"Roquefort is the extra-ponk French blue

cheese, yes?" said Arvo.

"Correct. Made from the milk of the sheep and ripened in caves. I read this on my phone's Cheese Data app."

"And the cunning Prankenstein has now done the hiding of this pranky-fuel somewhere on a massive-giant ship. It could be anywhere."

"Worse, he always secretes it in the small bits – it is likely to be in many places on board. He will do the prank mayhem."

"The ship could sink under the weight of jinks... we must find Soapy and make him have the tablets to stop the sleepwalks to find this Roquefort riot food."

Loogi then slapped the top of his head. "Eeooghhh!"

"What, Loogs? Have you found giant zit?"

"No, I have had bad-bad thought. The Royal Navy are on the way. This means military types will be boarding this ship to take away the pirates and to do the investigation into the hijack."

"Oh big-yikes! They will be searching the ship. What if they do the spotting of Prankenstein – they will be blasting him with naval cannons and explody missiles. Soapy will be totally conbooberated!"

"And even if Prankenstein evades them, he could be getting on board their navy ship – he will have the access to the rockets, bombs and torpedoes. Oh, big giant pooooo!"

Arvo stood up and banged down his fist on a desk. "Right, we must stop this disaster. We need to find Soapy most urgent. But because it is such giant ship, I think we should double our numbers – and ask Mincy and Horsehole to help."

Loogi's eyes nearly popped. "Whaaaaattt! Tell them about Prankenstein?"

"It's either that or we all end up at bottom of ocean on a pranky version of Titanic and then World War Three breaks out."

The Twince discovered Minty and Ursule in the games room where Minty was trying to beat Loogi's score at the Enigma Boom game. Ursule was sketching in her notebook. They found a quiet corner where they couldn't be overheard and then they explained the terrible truth of Soapy's Secret. The two girls listened agog, their mouths half-open, their eyes very open and their minds completely blown.

When Arvo finished speaking, Minty held up two hands as if she were surrendering. "Wait, wait, wait. Let me get this completely straight. Soapy, your best friend, transforms into a crazed prank-playing hairy monster when he eats cheese?"

Loogi nodded. "We have seen it with these own eyes. It was unreal and deep astonishing."

"But what does this Prankenstein actually do?" said Ursule, unable to hide how perplexed she was.

Arvo laughed. "What does he do? It may be the quicker to tell you what he does not do!"

The Twince then ran through a grisly catalogue of some of Prankenstein's most shocking pranks.

"This is how beefy armed hijackers were overcome in dark last night. Prankenstein has human-super strongness and faster speed than Usain Bolt with fireworks up bottom. He is double-treble crafty, silly, naughty, rascal and worse," said Loogi. "Mondo mischief monster."

"OK, I think we have the picture," said Minty. "What do we need to do?"

Arvo produced a deck plan of the ship. "We must find Soapy and do looking for cheese. We will split up and do deck each."

"All cheese must be thrown into sea," added Loogi. "We must somehow be raiding the ship's kitchens too."

13
Searching for Soapy

Minty took the top two decks, Ursule the next
two and Loogi decks five and six. Arvo meanwhile
went to the breakfast buffet. Here there were
tables covered in bowls of cereals, fruit, yogurt,
nuts, toast, jams, croissants, and juice, as well
as the hot section serving porridge, bacon, eggs,
sausages, beans, tomatoes and hash browns.

Arvo took the biggest plate he could find
then went to the steward serving the cooked
breakfasts. "Hello, good morning, I would like
some cheese please."

"Cheese for breakfast, sir? Wouldn't you rather
have a boiled egg or some crunchy pops?"

"No, I am from Estonia and we like cheese for
the brekkie." It helped that this was actually true.

The steward raised his eyebrows. "Well, er, all
right. We have some slices of Edam in the galley.

How many would you like?"

"Fifty."

The startled steward disappeared and came back with a small tower of cheese slices. He was further surprised to see Arvo walk straight out of the door with it. Three minutes later the boy returned with an empty plate and a smile.

"That cheese was being extra-yummy. Do you have any more?"

Minty meanwhile wandered round the top deck sniffing the air for Roquefort and calling, "Soapy!" An elderly lady stopped her and said, "Lost yer dog, eh, girl? Strange name for a pet, I must say. Mind you, I once had a cat called Strudel. I saw you were trying to sniff it out – smelly mutt is it? Or has it done a whoopsie on deck? Hang on, you can't take dogs on a cruise..." But Minty had run off.

Ursule had a little more luck. She possessed an excellent sense of smell and in the small library on Deck Three her nostrils detected something rather more whiffy than the average ancient paperback. She went along the shelves sniffing each row of books trying to locate where the pong was most intense. Ursule was concentrating so hard that she didn't see a smartly dressed gent looking at a guide to Tanzania and she bumped right into him.

"Oh, so sorry," she said.

"No problem. Well, I've heard of people judging a book by its cover before but never by its smell. I, er, hope you find something fragrant, miss."

She smiled and then had an idea. "Er, you don't happen to know where the food section is, do you?"

The gent pointed four rows back. "There's a couple of shelves of cookery books there."

Ursule thanked him then went over and scanned the books. *Wine Online, Italian Noodle Recipes, Great Hams of Peru, 100 ideas for Cabbage, 20-Second Puddings, The Ultimate Nog, A Beginner's Guide to Concealing Sprouts, Cheeses of Mongolia... Ha!*

She slid out the thin hardback book and there behind it was a small foil package. Ursule reached in, opened it out and was hit by the powerful, unmistakable hum of French Roquefort cheese. Not satisfied with her small triumph she continued to scan the different sections of the library.

Travel, Romance, Thrillers, Sport, Knitting,

Hovercraft Restoration, Humour. She stopped there and passed a finger over the different titles and subjects.

Jokes, Limericks, Hilarious Hockey Stories, Silly Poems, Tricks and Magic, Great Turkish Pranks of the '70s. It had to be. Once more, pulling out the book revealed a hidden package of cheese.

Loogi, on Deck Five, was concentrating on trying to find Soapy. His superior detective skills assured him that his friend would be curled up asleep somewhere. Prankenstein liked to operate at night as he would be too easily spotted during the day, especially on a busy ship. Loogi thought it was unlikely that he was snoozing in another passenger's cabin so he began to look at the various places along the deck that people could lie down in the sun or have a quiet read or nap.

He found a long line of sunloungers but these were mainly empty as it was still quite early in the day and many people on board would be still in bed after having been woken in the night by the hijack announcements. At the back of the deck were some padded chairs and a number of these were occupied by elderly passengers, most of whom were snoring with heads back and mouths open.

One chair, however, particularly interested Loogi. On this there was a small shape covered entirely by a large blanket. It was the shape of someone curled up asleep – someone most definitely boy-sized too. This would be his moment of triumph. He crept forward so as not to wake the other snoozers, took hold of a corner of the blanket and yanked it off calling, "Gotcha!"

It was Mrs Pew. She let out a piercing screech that probably woke the whole ship. Loogi ran.

Arvo had by this time taken all of the cheese in the buffet bar. It required five trips but it was now gone. His next plan was to get into the ship's main galley – the kitchen where he had been the night before and watched Soapy swallow a chunk of Double Gloucester and transform into a bristly trickster-beast. *Why, oh, why didn't we take away all the cheese last night when we had the chance?* Anyway, none of them had thought of it – they'd been too horrified at the thought of unleashing Prankenstein on a boat in the ocean.

When Arvo arrived at the galley he was surprised to see a large commotion inside with people climbing ladders and lots of shouting. He knocked on the door anyway. A white-aproned woman answered.

"Yes, may I help you?"

Arvo smiled. "I am doing a very difficult homework project about food preparation at sea and I wondered if possible that I might have very quick tour of the ship's kitchen to make a few notes. If I don't do good project my teacher says she will send me to evil tyrant headmaster."

"Oh dear, we can't have that... erm, I don't think it will do any harm if you have a quick tour. Come in."

Inside there were people standing on preparation surfaces reaching up as high as they could reach. They were trying to pull knives out of the ceiling.

"What happened?" said Arvo.

"We have no idea. When I arrived this morning every sharp utensil in the galley was stuck in the ceiling. It took us half an hour to get all the kebab skewers out. Perhaps some kind of magnetic surge caused it?"

Arvo nodded, but he knew otherwise. "Er, what is in these large refrigerators?" he asked, taking off his backpack and producing a notepad and pen

as well as furtively grabbing a handful of small objects.

The woman appeared pleased that he was interested in the work of the galley. "Oh, right, these are for dairy products: butter, milk, cream, yogurt, cheese as well as eggs and so on."

"Oh most of fascinating. Is it possible to see inside?"

The woman opened one of the large doors and as she did so Arvo quickly glanced around to check that no one was looking his way. He then quickly hurled a handful of goat teeth from his bone collection across the kitchen so that they clattered into stainless steel shelves and cupboards.

Everyone looked across to see what the sound was and in that moment Arvo reached into the fridge and stuffed a giant block of Captain's Crunch Cheddar into his bag.

Minty meanwhile was searching Deck Two. She crept into the Jazz Club and looked around. There wasn't really anywhere to hide cheese in the audience section where there were just rows of chairs so she climbed up onto the stage where there were black cases no doubt containing trumpets, saxophones and other instruments. First, she raised the lid of the large glossy grand piano. Inside Minty expected to see lots of wires and wooden hammers. Instead she saw lots of water and fish. There was even an octopus at the bottom. At first, she was so surprised that her brain just turned into cotton wool. Then it sprang into life.

"Prankenstein! So this is the kind of thing he does."

Carefully she went over to the instrument cases and opened a small one that should have contained a violin. Inside was a jellyfish. Next she opened a large tuba case, fearing the worst. This did not contain a slimy sea-creature but instead a pile of silky looking clothes. Minty picked one of them up: bloomers. She quickly shut the case.

The other bags and containers on the stage revealed a stinky collection including seaweed, squid, shellfish, some unidentified jelly-like eggs and a pile of rotting fish-heads. But no cheese.

Using her keen sense of smell, Ursule had by this time tracked down nine small foil packages of Roquefort. She had also discovered some very odd things on Deck Four: every seat in the ship's small cinema was smeared with treacle, the weights in the Fitness Centre had been replaced with pies and the treadmills in the gym had all been set to 'Nitro Zoom' level.

She now went outside and stood against the rail overlooking the rolling water of the Indian Ocean. Turning her back to the sea she made sure that no one was watching then began to flick the small parcels of cheese over the side of the ship. A figure appeared and for a moment she froze. It was Arvo. He nodded knowingly, glanced around, took off his backpack, lifted it up to the top of the railing then tipped out the 4kg block of cheddar, which fell into the water with a resounding splash. He wondered what the dolphins would make of it.

Ursule smiled and leant over to him. "How do you dispose of cheese on a cruise liner?" He shrugged, unsure what she meant.

"Caerphilly."

He still had no idea what she meant.

A few moments later Minty arrived, followed by Loogi.

"This whole ship has been pranked to pieces,"

she said. "The kiddies' paddling pool is full of gravy."

"I found eels in the hairdressing salon," said Loogi. "And according to the menu in the Pacific Restaurant, today's special is fish guts on toast."

Ursule and Arvo shared what they'd discovered of Prankenstein's work too and wondered what he'd done in the engine room or to the ship's navigation system.

"It is grisly to be imagining," said Loogi, "But what is cheese finding situation?"

"I've found some of the Roquefort," said Ursule, but there could be hundreds more pieces hidden on the ship."

Arvo shook his head. "I have collected oodles of cheeses and lobbed them all into sea but it is being hopeless – there are still kilos of it on board. We cannot do this."

Minty said, "What about finding Soapy?"

Loogi held out his hands. "I have tried

but again, ship is too large. I found Mrs Spew and frightened her large-time but no Soapy. It would take days to search, and days we do not have. Prankenstein is winning."

Arvo looked up and pointed out to sea, where a grey ship was approaching. "Most correct. Here is Royal Navy."

14
Naval nightmare

The Royal Navy Patrol Cruiser HMS Penge
drew up alongside *The Queen of the Ocean,* which
slowed to a halt. Forty-six sailors were transferred
to the liner to begin the investigation, take away
the hijackers and comb the huge cruise liner for
anything dangerous that the pirates might have
planted. They were also requested by Captain Rice
to try and find a missing boy, Pugh Thompson,
whose mother wouldn't stop pestering him. The
captain had enough problems with reports of 283
pranks that had been carried out on board during
the previous night by a mystery joker.

The two sets of twins were ordered to return
to their cabins, as were all of the other passengers,
while the search was carried out. Arvo and Loogi
just had to wait.

"What if Prankenstein gets onto that Navy

Cruiser?" said Arvo.

"Do sailors like cheese? They like grog, I think. What is grog?"

"Of course, this could work out better than we think. Navy search party may find Soapy."

"They may also find Prankenstein. What then?"

"Am refusing to do the imagining of that..."

It was Midshipman Ryan Denton who made the discovery at 2.18pm. He immediately reported to his commanding officer.

"I found something odd in one of the lifeboats, Sir."

"Yes? What is it?"

"A sleeping boy, Sir."

"Oh, right, I see. Anything else?"

"He was sleeping on a pillow stuffed with cheese, Sir."

Soapy was returned to his parents with a monumental fuss and everyone rejoiced. His mother finally began to calm down when the Navy search was completed and the ship was declared free from hijack threat (although the sailors did report discovering some more very odd things and a curious number of small parcels of Roquefort). The Twince, along with all of the other passengers were allowed out of their cabins and the boys wasted no time in searching out Minty and Ursule to discuss what they should do next.

"We should celebrate, for sure. I have some Maltesers," said Minty.

"Not so quick with chocs yet, I think," said Loogi. "Soapy has returned but there is still cheese on board this boat."

"But I thought you said as long as Soapy stays away from it then we're all safe from Prankenstein," said Ursule.

"That is correct but Soapy has annoying habit of sleepwalking much," said Arvo, "and Prankenstein is turbo crafty. He wants to return each night."

"But Soapy has pills to stop him sleepwalking, doesn't he?" asked Minty.

Loogi nodded. "Yes, and we must make double sure he takes them. Soapy may not even know what he did last night. We need to see him, pronto – we must sneak into his room."

Sneaking into Soapy's cabin was easier said than done. There was still a squad of Navy sailors aboard guarding the ship and Mrs Thompson was also on patrol. Arvo had a good idea, however.

"I will go and see Mr and Mrs T and ask them in their cabin how Soapy is doing. I will be pummelling them with the questions and in that time you three can do the sneaky nip into Soapy's cabin."

They agreed it was a top plan and they set it into motion immediately. Arvo put on his best polite, 'concerned' face and went to see the Thompsons while Loogi and the girls quietly knocked on Soapy's door.

"Go away!" he said.

They went in. He was lying face down on his bed holding a cushion over his head. "Sorry, Soapy," said Loogi, "but we need to tell you the thing most important." He just groaned.

"You know that you became the Prankenstein last night?"

"OF COURSE I KNOW, I HAVE THE WORST HEADACHE IN THE WORLD AND ANYWAY YOU WERE WITH ME!" He sat up and nearly shrieked. "Minty and Ursule? Oh, er, I thought it

was just the Twince, I er, er…" His eyes flicked
to Loogi.

"Yes, they know – we had to be telling them."

"But why?" said Soapy, "It was a secret!"

Minty and Ursule shuffled and looked down at
their feet.

Loogi sat down on the bed. "Listen, your plan
worked last night and you rescued your mum and
biffed the pirates but Prankenstein was also doing
his naughty trick of hiding cheese."

Minty joined in. "We tried to find all the cheese
and find you so you won't become Prankenstein
again. You did do an awful lot of scandalous pranks
across the ship."

Soapy perked up. "Did I? Ooh, tell me... No, wait – it wasn't me you know. I never remember what Prankenstein does – he's a different person." He gave the girls a hard stare. "But you won't tell a living soul about this, will you? My mum would mince me alive if she knew I was doing a Jekyll and Hyde act."

Ursule and Minty shook their heads. "We promise."

"OK, well, I just hope that that horrid Spewy man got properly pranked – that would make it all worthwhile."

Loogi continued. "Look, Soapy, there is Royal Navy here with big military cruiser – full of rockets and torpedoes. We must make sure that Prankenstein is not let out again on this cruise."

Soapy rubbed his eyes. "Of course – it won't happen. Even if there's cheese still hidden aboard I'll just take my special pills to stop me sleepwalking." He began to pull open his bedside drawers. "Now, where are they?"

15
On guard

Soapy pulled the small wooden drawer right out. "They were definitely here yesterday. I've been taking the pills every night and I haven't sleepwalked on the voyage at all."

Loogi pulled a hand down his face. "But now they are gone: Prankenstein's doing for sure."

"They might just have fallen out," said Minty. "We'll help you look."

The four of them searched the small cabin thoroughly but there was no sign of the red tablets.

"It's not hopeless, though," said Soapy. "My mum has spare packets."

He gave his hair a quick comb, put on a new T-shirt and went across to his parents' cabin. He returned five minutes later with Arvo, his face grey.

"My mum can't find them. Prankenstein's probably thrown them in the sea."

The five children met in the games room once more. Soapy's mum had come to give his room another search and he and the others told her that they'd better get out of her way. She hardly noticed as they slipped out.

The five knew that they simply had to stop Soapy sleepwalking that night or disaster could result.

"I have plan," said Arvo. "There are four of us, not including Soapy. We can divide up the night-time and each patrol the corridor outside his room. Two hours each."

Minty nodded rapidly. "OK, we'll fix up a timetable and sneak out of our rooms – good idea."

"There is problem with this plan," said Loogi.

"You mean we might be discovered in the corridor by the staff or Royal Navy?" said Ursule.

"Well, yes, that as well. I was meaning Soapy – what if he comes out of the room, sleepwalking? How do we stop him? What do we do?"

Soapy laughed. "Hey, come on – it can't be that hard. I'm just a kid. Wake me up or just shove me back in bed."

Arvo twisted a lip. "I fear my brainy brother may be right. I have heard stories before of dangers of waking sleepwalking peoples."

"Ooh, what stories?" said Minty.

"It can be dangerous – you never know how they react. They might even attack you if they are having bad dreamy-time."

Loogi nodded. "Yes, best to be carrying weapon for self-defence, I think."

Soapy's jaw fell. "What? Are you going to smack me with baseball bats?"

Ursule put up a finger. "Rolled up magazines should do it – and we'll have something to read if we're bored."

Arvo stood up. "Agreed."

Soapy stood up. "Oi, I haven't agreed to anything."

Loogi put a hand on his shoulder. "Sorry, Soapy, but Prankenstein cannot be unleashed again. We must biff if necessary."

At 3am in the middle of that night, Arvo snuck out of his cabin and headed down the corridor towards Soapy's door. Outside in the gloom he saw Ursule sitting and reading a book.

"Hi," he said in a heavy whisper. "All quiet here?"

She stood up. "Yes, nothing to report, except that my bottom aches. I decided on this giant volume of 'Contemporary African Sculptures' I found in the library to whack him with but he's still asleep."

Arvo nodded, producing a magazine from his back pocket. "Good. I have 'Junior Bone Collector Monthly'. It is 164 pages so handy for the clobber."

Ursule stretched and yawned. "Right, well, I hope you have a quiet patrol like I did. I'm off to bed now – hopefully Minty will be here at five."

Arvo sat outside Soapy's door in the half-light wondering how he was going to stay awake. He was already drifting a little and it had always been a problem with him. His mind cast back to the previous year when he and Loogi had sat in Soapy's bedroom, carrying out their first experiment to discover if Soapy was indeed Prankenstein. He recalled a big pot of coffee and a giant hoagie but his mind was going blank... he was dropping off and simply couldn't stop himself.

A sudden clunk jolted him awake. *Soapy's door?*

Arvo looked across and saw it was still closed. Instead a shadow loomed over him. "What is your name and could you please explain what you are doing?"

It was a uniformed Royal Navy sailor.

"Erm, um, I am Arvo. I am just having the snooze," mumbled Arvo unconvincingly.

The large shaven-headed man raised an eyebrow. "But why here? You should be in your cabin, young man. I'm going to have to ask you to return to it right now for security purposes."

Arvo knew there was no arguing. He took one last glance at Soapy's door behind the beefy seaman and stood up.

What now?

At that moment there was a click and Soapy's door flew open with tremendous force. The man standing right outside it was knocked clean off

his feet. Arvo watched with shock as he toppled across the corridor and cracked his head on a door handle before dropping to the floor, unconscious. Arvo gaped.

Out of the door emerged Soapy

Thompson. His eyes were open but his face was unseeing. He was walking in heavy, clumping strides as if he were some kind of robot.

"Soapy! Stop!" called Arvo, stepping over the large body next to him. "It's me, your friend. Or is it I? Anyway, it's Arvo – wake up!"

Soapy's expression registered nothing. Arvo clicked his fingers and waved hands in front of Soapy's face but still his friend kept on walking.

This is total bonkers thought Arvo, who then remembered the magazine. He rolled it up and gave Soapy a light tap on the arm. Nothing happened. He did another, this time on the nose, but still the boy continued in his lumbering trance down the corridor. Arvo took a deep breath then whacked him full force over the head. Soapy did not even blink. He just kept moving towards the exit door, staring, silent, a junior zombie.

Arvo had to stop him. He put down the magazine and stood in Soapy's path, bracing himself, his arm out like a police officer holding up traffic.

"Stop, you noodle, stop!"

Soapy did not stop. Like a bulldozer he simply shoved his friend down and trampled on him as he reached the exit door. The last thing Arvo recalled was a toe up his left nostril as the sleepwalking boy disappeared into the night.

16
Zanzibar

That night the escorted cruise liner reached
its destination, the African island of Zanzibar.
It docked with great care in the dark and a large
gangplank was lowered onto the quay.

Inside the ship, just before dawn, Minty crept
down the corridor towards Soapy's cabin. She was
very surprised to see two bodies on the floor. One
was evidently Arvo. She bent down and gently
tugged at his collar.

"Wake up, wake up. What happened?"

As Arvo gradually came to his senses, Minty
scampered along the corridor to Soapy's room.

She pushed the door open and gave a gasp.

Soapy was in there fast asleep.

Arvo shakily stood up and spoke with a croak.
"He escaped... he bashed the sailor then just
trod all over me... He's gone, this is terrible-bad-

terrible... Oh my neck..."

Minty helped him walk. "Look, I don't know what happened here but Soapy's not gone – he's fast asleep in his room."

"He cannot be – he went out last night onto the ship – Prankenstein is free! Ouch, ooh."

Minty quietly pushed Soapy's door open again and pointed to their sleeping friend. "See."

Arvo stared. "But, what? But..."

"Maybe you bashed into that sailor in the night and imagined all this. Anyway, we must get out of here – he could wake up any time now and arrest us."

Arvo nodded and the two of them scurried to their rooms.

Soapy was awoken at 8.15am by an announcement from the Captain.

"GOOD MORNING. WE DOCKED DURING THE NIGHT AT THE PORT OF ZANZIBAR AND ALL PASSENGERS ARE WELCOME TO DISEMBARK FOR A VISIT TO THE CITY. THE SHIP WILL BE HERE FOR 16 HOURS. OUR ROYAL NAVY

GUARDS WILL SOON BE LEAVING US BUT
IN THE MEANTIME THEY WOULD LIKE
TO INTERVIEW A YOUNG MAN POSSIBLY
CALLED NERVO, OR ARGO. THANK YOU."

Soapy was not listening; he was too busy
rolling around with an ogre of a headache.

Soapy's dad was very keen to go and explore
Zanzibar. The Thompsons and the Twince were
waiting in a line of people to disembark from the
ship down the gangplank. It was a slow process
because further ahead three Royal Navy
sailors were checking
everybody before they
left the liner.

"It has a fascinating
history, I was reading,"
Mr Thompson said.
"Zanzibar was once
East Africa's main
slave-trading port,
and there are
also all sorts of
interesting old
buildings and

sights."

Mrs Thompson looked a little more doubtful. "Well, it will be nice to get off the ship onto dry land, especially after the shenanigans of the past few days but remember – especially you three boys – all these places are full of dangerous tropical germs so don't touch anything unless you have to, especially at the markets, and if you do touch anything spray yourself with anti-bacterial fluid. Got that?"

The only one of the boys who nodded was Loogi. Soapy wasn't listening because his headache was still pounding away and Arvo was too busy anxiously watching the big Navy men whom they were now approaching. With horror, he recognised one of them as the brawny shaven-headed sailor who Soapy had knocked out in the night. The man was checking every face and, to make things worse, he had a large red lump on the side of his head.

Arvo grabbed his brother, held him back and whispered, "What shall we do? This is sailor-brute who Soapy bopped last night. He will recognise me for sure and then I will be put in Navy Jail with chains and the stinky rat."

Loogi slipped a floppy sun hat out of his pocket

and gave it to Arvo. "Here, put this on, stay hidden as possible and leave this to me."

Arvo was very confused but there was no time to ask what the plan was. He put on the silly hat, pulled up his collar and shrank down with bent knees as the family approached the checkpoint at the top of the gangplank.

The three stern military men scanned each face of the people in front of the Thompsons then let them pass. To everyone's surprise, Loogi made a quick shuffle forward and walked out in front of Soapy's mum and dad, smiling and nodding at the sailors.

"Oi, you, stop!" The burly man put out an arm and grabbed Loogi by the shoulder. The other two held up the rest of the queue behind him.

"You look very familiar to me. Is your name Nervo, or Ahso, or possibly Evo?"

Loogi continued to give an unruffled smile. "No, my name

is Loogi."

Soapy's mum inevitably stepped forward and went into her lawyer mode. "Is there a problem here? What is the hold-up?"

Another of the sailors spoke. "We have suspicion, ma'am, that this young man may have been involved in an assault last night on one of our crew."

Mrs Thompson's shoulders bristled. "That's a very serious allegation. Do you have any evidence?"

The man hesitated. "Well, Midshipman Denton here has a nasty lump on his head."

"Really? He could have done that walking down stairs or going to the toilet. Are there any witnesses?"

Denton nodded. "Yeah, me – and I clearly remember his face. He was acting suspiciously in one of the ship's corridors last night at about 3.20am."

Soapy's mum turned to Loogi. "Is this true? Were you in one of the corridors at 3.20 this morning?"

Loogi didn't flinch. "Of course not. I was fast sleeping. Why would I be in the corridor then? This is total truth and I swear it on Bible, Koran, Oxford English Dictionary and Harry Potter."

Everyone in the queue was watching and all could see that Loogi was not telling a lie. Even Soapy was following the scene with fascination.

Mrs Thompson cleared her throat. "Does that satisfy you? If you have no actual evidence or other witnesses then I demand you let us pass. This cruise has been disrupted enough as it is. Goodbye." The waiting passengers gave a brief cheer as Soapy's mum bustled past the sheepish sailors, shepherding the three boys through as well, including a remarkably small, hatted Arvo.

Zanzibar was hot and busy and noisy. Crowds of souvenir sellers who had been waiting for the cruise liner to arrive scuttled round the passengers who now mingled with the other tourists on the large island. Soapy's mum told them to go away even though Mr Thompson and the boys wanted a closer look at what they were selling. Soapy's dad unfolded a map of the town, Zanzibar City.

"I think we should go and see The House of Wonders first, then have a look around the old town for some lunch."

"What is House of Wonders, I wonder?" said

Arvo, who had now taken off the ridiculous hat and grown back to his normal size. "What do you think, Soapy?"

"What?" he mumbled, his eyes half-closed.

Loogi looked at his friend and realised that the Twince had been so busy avoiding the sailors that they hadn't really paid any attention to Soapy. "Is that sleepiness or headache?" he said.

"A horrible, horrible headache," said Soapy.

Arvo made sure that Mr and Mrs Thompson could not hear. "Ah, so perhaps I am not being so stupid after all. I told you that I remember Soapy sleepwalk-biffing both me and that Navy guy last night. It was not a dream like Minty says."

"Oh, multi-yikes," said Loogi. "So Prankenstein was on loose last night. I wonder what he got up to? Do you remember anything Soapy?"

"I don't care," he groaned.

In front, Mr Thompson stopped and turned the map around a few times. "Er, I think it's this way. Or it could be that way," he said, pointing down a street of dusty stone buildings.

Soapy's mum shook her head. "We're only a hundred yards from the boat and we're lost already…"

As the pair of them squabbled, Arvo looked up and saw some familiar faces approaching from a busy street. It was Minty and Ursule with their parents. Loogi was very impressed that their dad had a waxed moustache and tweed shorts. Their mum was very tall with a pink dress and a ludicrous quantity of teeth. They smiled a lot and said hello and everyone was properly introduced.

"Where are you orf to, then?" said the girls' mother smiling excessively.

"Well, we're, er, trying to find the House of Wonders," said Soapy's dad, turning the map again.

"Oh, we were going to go there," said Minty, "But this local fellow said that it's been taken over by monkeys who are throwing fruit at anyone who approaches."

"And you believed him?" said Mrs Thompson, her eyebrows high.

The girls' father laughed. "Yes, I suppose we did – especially when he told us that the city market has run out of fruit as well. Jolly strange, eh?"

"We're going to the Turkish Fort instead," said Ursule. "Why don't you come with us?"

Soapy's mum gave a half smile. "Thank you but we want to go and see this House of Wonders for ourselves. Is it this way?"

The girls' mother pointed up the busy street and told them to turn right at the top. "Watch out for flying pomegranates, though, ha ha."

17
The House of Melons

The House of Wonders was a lot further away than the Thompsons expected.

"That's because we've gone the wrong way about thirty-four times," said Mrs Thompson who was by now getting seriously grumpy.

When they arrived they could see the cruise liner not far away.

"Hmmm, I think we may have gone the long way around, sorry," said Mr Thompson, finally folding away the map.

The house was an impressive old palace covered in long balconies held up by pillars. It was on the edge of some gardens facing the sea. There were quite a number of police officers about, Soapy noticed.

"Well, I am not seeing any monkeys," said Arvo looking up and down the front of the

building. They started to walk towards the entrance when an overripe peach came winging through the air from the roof. It splattered onto Loogi's leg.

"Ugh," he said. "Those things have the big stones inside and anyway, I am preferring nectarine."

Before anyone could reply, a volley of fruit was launched from the top verandah by a cackling troupe of what looked like small baboons. Mr Thompson took the first hit as a half-eaten banana smeared across his ear. Soapy was whacked by a mango and Arvo was hit twice, once with a manky fig and then right in the mouth with a juicy apricot.

"Come on, run!" shouted Mr Thompson covering his head with the map as a cluster of purple grapes pinged off his bottom.

"Oh, do stop shouting, really," called Soapy's mum. "It's only a bit of fruit. We'll do the British thing and walk away in a dignified manner." She had barely spoken the words when a very large watermelon came sailing across from one of the upper balconies. Mr Thompson saw it and ducked. It hit his wife between the shoulder blades, sending her flying into a prickly bush.

Soapy and his dad tried to pull her out while

Arvo and Loogi retreated behind a tree saying that they weren't British anyway. She was still breathing but her white cotton top was now pink and green and wet and her hair was full of spikes like some kind of ninja wig.

"We'd better get you out of here, dear," said Mr Thompson, but she couldn't stand up. The melon had winded her and she was only half-conscious. Soapy didn't need to think who had given the monkeys all of the ammo.

Mr Thompson grabbed her under the armpits and persuaded Soapy to hold her ankles while Arvo and Loogi emerged from their hiding place to pick up her handbag and hat. Meanwhile the army of apes launched another attack, this time with plums.

"At least they're not lobbing pineapples," said Soapy, heaving his mum away from the house.

"Is pumpkin a fruit?" asked Loogi. "That would be bad."

"They would need gorilla for that," said Arvo.

A policeman rushed up to help but just as everyone thought they were safe his helmet was knocked off by what appeared to be a cannonball.

"Quick, quick, quick, sirs," gabbled the officer.

"They have started on the coconuts."

Everyone agreed that the excursion to Zanzibar had not been a great success. Mrs Thompson had been put on a stretcher and taken back to the cruise liner where the ship's doctor had treated her melon wounds.

"Did you notice the name of the ship?" said Soapy when he finally sat down with the Twince in their cabin, all of them having showered and changed clothes.

"Queen of the Ocean?" said Loogi.

"Well it was. It's been painted again. It's now *The Queen of the Onion*. Prankenstein sure was busy last night."

Arvo flopped down on his bed. "We are only halfway round this cruise of pranks. We must find a way to stop Prankenstein or he will do us all in."

Soapy held out his hands. "But the sleeping pills are gone."

At that moment there was a knock on the door. It was Minty and Ursule. The Foolish Five were together again.

"We heard the monkeys bombed you with fruit," said Minty. "Well, we did warn you."

"Apart from nearly killing us, it was quite funny," said Soapy.

"Is your mum OK?" asked Ursule, thoughtfully.

"I think so. She's being kept in the sick bay for observation. They keep finding kiwi pips embedded in her chin."

Minty looked at Arvo. "I need to apologise. I'm sorry I didn't believe you about last night. So Prankenstein did get out and visit the city."

Arvo held up a hand. "It's OK. Did you come across other examples of his handiwork on the island?"

"We heard that the fountain outside the Town Hall is now full of beer."

"And that the library is roaming with crocodiles."

"And that Prankenstein electrified the toilet seats in the Grand Hotel."

"Shocking."

The four twins laughed at that one but Soapy let out a long groan. "What's up?" said Arvo.

"What's up? WHAT'S UP? I used to be thrilled by these pranks and the idea of playing tricks on so many people but I haven't told you what I heard earlier, when I went to visit my mum in the sick bay."

"What?" Everyone's expression fell to solemn.

"I crept in there quietly because I didn't want to disturb

my mum in case she was asleep. She was in a bed with one of those curtains round it and my dad was in there with her talking. They didn't know I had come in and I could overhear what they were saying."

The Twince and the twins listened intently as Soapy gave a sigh.

"They were talking about the pranks and about me. My dad was saying, 'Have you noticed how these pranks seem to follow our family around? First at home and then our town, then when my brother came over from the States and now here, in Africa…' Mum answered that it clearly wasn't her and it wasn't him so it must be something to do with me – or Arvo and Loogi."

The Twince looked at each other and gulped. Soapy continued.

"They talked about having CCTV installed or fitting me with a tracking device. They even discussed paying for a private detective to follow me about!"

Minty bit her lip, "So they are on to you?"

"Well, it's getting dangerous. There's also the ship's crew watching us and the Navy and The Pews and probably all the other passengers as well. What if they catch Prankenstein? They would probably throw him in the sea... I've only got a 50 metres badge – I'll drown!"

Loogi pulled out a small pad and his crossword pen. "We cannot let our friend go to watery grave or end up in cruisy prison. We must formulate an excellent plan to stop Prankenstein now."

"Agreed," they all said. But Soapy had his doubts. They had tried so many plans in the past and Prankenstein had foiled them all.

18
The prank alarm

The Foolish Five came up with nineteen plans but they all agreed that eighteen of them were never going to work. The only good one was Ursule's. She explained it to the group.

"Right, the key is to stop Soapy getting out when he sleepwalks. My plan is that he isn't allowed to escape because he's locked in. The special part is that he isn't in his own room. At lights out, Soapy sneaks across here to the Twince's room with his mattress and sleeps on the floor. When he is asleep, Arvo and Loogi lock the door from the inside and tie up the latch so it cannot be easily undone. Furthermore you attach a string to Soapy's toe and tie the other end through the wardrobe and to a collection of noisy objects – a prank alarm. If it goes off you wake him."

"How?" said Arvo. "I couldn't do it before."

"Throw a bucket of water over his head. Never fails."

They all agreed it was a fine plan. The enterprising girls went off to borrow string, scissors and a bucket while

Arvo and Loogi discussed how best to fix the door latch so a sleepwalker wouldn't be able to open it. Soapy snuck into the buffet to borrow some spoons for the prank alarm. On the way back he called into the sick bay to see how his mum was doing.

"Much better, thank you," she said. "I'll be allowed out this evening. I hope you are being good, Pugh."

"Er, of course," he said, trying to hide the bulge of five spoons in his pocket.

"It's just that, well, all these pranks happening again. I know you couldn't possibly have armed two hundred monkeys with fruit on an African island or filled a paddling pool with gravy but it is very, very odd that these incidents happen wherever we are around, don't you think?" She looked him hard in the eye.

"The pranks are astounding, Mum, but you're right that a boy like me couldn't possibly do them."

"Hmmm, but what about three boys?"

"The Twince haven't done anything, Mum!"

"And what about you?"

"It wasn't me, Mum, honest – it was someone else."

She looked at him hard again. "But who? But who? We just *have* to find out."

At precisely 10.05pm Ursule's plan swung into action. She was disappointed that she couldn't be there to see it but she had checked out the string alarm and door locking system and approved of both. The girls had said goodnight and good luck an hour before but now the plan rested with the Twince and Soapy.

A coded knock on the boy's door revealed Soapy in pyjamas with his mattress. He placed it between the two beds on the floor then lay down. The three spoke in whispers as Loogi tied some string to Soapy's left big toe.

"What if it pulls my toe off?" he said.

"We'll just have to risk it," said Arvo.

"What if I need a pee in the night?"

"Hold it in."

"What if the ship is sinking and we can't get out because of your weird knot on the door lock?"

"It's OK, we can open it."

"What if my mum and dad go in my room and find it empty?"

"They'll think you're sleepwalking again – they'll find you in here, safe."

"So how do we explain my mattress being here?"

"It was a… cargo sleepwalk – new kind that scientists have discovered. We will say a girl in New Zealand once carried a plank twelve miles in the night."

"They won't believe you."

"SOAPY, SHUT UP AND GO SLEEP!"

Loogi threaded the string through their wardrobe handle and tied the other end to the five metal spoons. There was plenty of slack so the spoons rested on the floor.

"OK, Soapy get up and pretend you're sleepwalking."

"I'm asleep."

The alarm worked. The spoons clanked against the handle when the string was pulled.

Meanwhile Arvo finished pouring the last of 129 cupfuls of cold water into the bucket that Minty had borrowed from a cleaning cupboard. He added a bag of ice for good measure.

"All ready," he said. The Twince climbed into bed and put out the lights.

"Sleep well. No sleepwalking. No pranks," said Arvo.

"No talking," said Loogi.

"I'm still asleep," said Soapy, giggling at his own joke.

There was a few seconds silence then someone burped.

The three boys did not go to sleep for a long time, but eventually the roll of the ship and the faint hum of its vast engines sent them off. It was the same story two decks above where Minty and Ursule lay in their beds too nervous to drop off. All five were thinking the same thoughts as they drifted into slumber. *Will it work? Can Prankenstein be stopped?*

19
Good morning?

Some mornings you wake up fresh and rested and feeling wonderful. Others you wake up feeling like you've been in a wrestling match. This morning was not like either of those. This morning was upside down.

Loogi woke up first. His head felt hot and dizzy. He rubbed his eyes and saw a number of peculiar sights. First, the ceiling was now carpeted. But even stranger than that, all the furniture was stuck to it. He looked out of the porthole and saw that the sky was at the bottom and the sea was at the top. *Whhaaatttt?*

Only after ten seconds or so did he realise that he was hanging upside down. He was tied to the top of the wardrobe by two loops made from socks around his ankles and fixed with string.

Between his toes were two spoons. He wriggled and thrashed around and fell with a thump, joining his brother who had seemingly dropped down from the same position earlier and then fallen asleep again. Typical Arvo.

Soapy was not there.

"Wake up, wake up dozy boy!" Loogi shook his brother but all of the blood was rushing out of his head and he flopped down in a kind of peculiar slow-motion faint. Lying back on the carpet he came round again and opened his eyes. He was staring under Arvo's bed and there, hidden from sight were four small foil packages, including one that had been opened.

Oh no, not again...

Arvo surfaced, rubbing his eyes and looking round, trying to piece together what had happened. Loogi sat on his bed and made it clear.

"Prankenstein must have hidden cheese in here, under our beds last time he was about.

When we did searching of ship we never thought of looking here. He's just too clever."

Arvo blinked. "So he didn't even need to sleepwalk out of the room. He had cheese in the cabin all along..."

"He pranked us, bust open our lock knot easily and just went out to do more prank terrors. Who knows what shocking things await out there."

"So, how did he prank us, exactly?" said Arvo looking around.

"Atch, we were hanging upside down from the wardrobe, you case of the nut!"

"Not I, you maybe... Perhaps I am not so easily pranked, ha."

At that moment there was a coded knock on the door.

"Soapy?" said Arvo. "More like Manky and Aerosol – I mean Minty and Ursule."

He stood up and headed for the door. However he didn't notice the string round his toe. Or that it was tucked behind the bed and up the back of the wardrobe. Or that it was tied to a bucket on the wardrobe.

As Arvo swung open the cabin door the string pulled taut. He was soaked by twelve litres of water, as were the two girls waiting to come in.

"Well," said Minty. "I was just about to ask if the plan worked. I think this may have answered it.

"It's OK," laughed Loogi. "My brother is not so easily pranked."

The four of them cleaned up the wet mess as well as they could and then sat down to decide what to do. They discussed going to see if Soapy would be in his room but they all agreed that he would be.

"With a headache," said Arvo.

"And total unaware of what mayhem he – Prankenstein – has done," added Loogi.

"I wonder what he has done?" said Minty.

"Perhaps it's time we told everyone the truth then maybe Prankenstein can be stopped."

There was a moment of silence as they all thought about the consequences of revealing Soapy's shocking secret to the world.

Then the ship's piercing emergency hooter rang out shattering the quiet.

"I think we are about to find out what he did last night," said Ursule.

20
Full speed ahead

"THIS IS AN EMERGENCY ANNOUNCEMENT,
AN EMERGENCY ANNOUNCEMENT.
ALL CREW REPORT TO YOUR STATIONS.
SECURITY TEAM RED ALERT. REPEAT,
ALL CREW REPORT TO YOUR STATIONS.
SECURITY TEAM RED ALERT. PASSENGERS
PLEASE DO NOT BE ALARMED BUT
STAY CALM AND STAY WHERE YOU ARE.
REPEAT, STAY WHERE YOU ARE."

It was hard to hear the message over the screaming of the siren. A moment later the door flew open. It was Mr Thompson.

"Have you seen Soapy? He's not in his cabin."

They shook their heads and he dashed off, leaving the door open. Outside the four kids could see a red light flashing in the corridor and people rushing about with wide eyes. Everyone was gabbling or shouting. Some were wrestling with lifejackets.

"I thought we were supposed to stay calm," said Minty.

The two pairs of twins decided that they needed to do two things. One, find out what was going on, and two, locate Soapy. They joined the scurrying throng in the corridor, went through the exit and headed up onto the outside deck where they could see the ship properly. The first thing that they noticed was the noise and the wind. It flapped their hair into their eyes.

"Whoah," said Arvo. "This is rough and windy much."

Minty disagreed. "No, look out there at the sea – it's not rough at all. No white water."

"It's the ship," said Ursule, holding onto a rail as a spray of salt water shot up and went over their heads. "It's zooming along."

The Twince looked down and they could see she was right. There was a great surge of angled seawater trailing back from the giant ship as it blasted across the ocean.

"What's going on?"

The four of them ran along the deck trying to find a steward. One rushed past with a handful of lifejackets and Loogi grabbed his arm.

"Please, what is happening?"

The man's eyes were darting round and his breath was short. "Er, erm, look just put one of these on, all of you. There's going to be an announcement to do so in a minute anyway."

"But why is the ship going so fast?" said Minty.

They could see the man was in two minds, unsure what to say.

"Er, erm."

"Hey, come on, we need to be knowing – if emergency," said Arvo.

The man nodded rapidly. "Someone – some*thing* – has taken over the bridge, tied up the captain and senior officers and locked the doors to the navigation and control areas. He... it... it's taken over the ship."

"But why is it going so fast?" asked Ursule

"I don't know – I didn't think it could go this fast. I've been working on cruise liners for twenty years and never seen one go half as fast as this! I must go, sorry – good luck."

He ran off and the four put on their orange

lifejackets.

"So Soapy is still Prankenstein and he's controlling the ship," said Minty. "But why hasn't he turned back to a boy?"

"Perhaps he scoffed extra cheese?" said Arvo. "Anyways, we know Prankenstein better than anyone here. Maybe we are ones that can stop him."

"But where is he heading in such a rush?" said Ursule.

Loogi started running up some steps to the upper decks. "I think I know – follow me." The two pairs of twins dashed past swarms of terrified passengers and finally reached the upper observation deck where there was the best view of the ship. They all turned to the front, the wind blasting their faces.

No one said a word. From here, it was very clear exactly where the ship was headed. There in front of them about six miles away was a small island. The island was dominated by a great black menacing mountain, thousands of metres high and out of which great billows of fiery evil grey smoke were rising high, high into the blue above.

21
Grounded

For a moment the four children just stood and stared. They were heading straight for a rumbling volcano at maximum speed.

"OK," said Minty, "We need to stay calm and think what to do."

"Aaarrrrggghhhhh!" said Arvo. "Sorry, I and volcanoes do not get along."

Ursule ignored him. "If Prankenstein has locked himself in the bridge and has control of the ship it's going to be tough for us to stop him but maybe we could distract him?"

Loogi nodded. "Ah yes, if he sees us at the window then maybe he will be recognising us and that will put him off the wild speed dash."

"Hey," said Arvo, who had now calmed down. "Look." He pointed down and saw that someone was attempting to lower one of the ship's lifeboats.

"It's Spewy!"
said Minty. They
walked to the rail
for a closer look
and could see
the unmistakable
bulk of Mr Pew
and his wife trying
to sneak away in
a lifeboat.

"Do we try and stop him or try and stop
Prankenstein?" said Ursule.

They all agreed that stopping the prank-
monster was more urgent and so they began
descending the metal steps that led towards the
bridge at the front of the ship. However, when
they reached the deck below two security men
blocked the way. Next to them was one of the
ship's officers in his white uniform, his face red
and glistening as he gabbled into a walkie-talkie.

"For goodness' sake, Winstanley, you're the
Chief Engineer, there's got to be a way to slow the
ship down from the engine room… What? Why?…
Well, just cut the engines, then… You can't?
It's not possible for the engines to be going this

fast – we're doing 57 knots! It could only happen if they've been tampered with... They *have* been tampered with? Oh no..."

Minty told one of the security men that Mr and Mrs Pew were trying to steal a lifeboat. "You what? We can't launch lifeboats at this speed! That's why we haven't abandoned the ship. Where are they?"

The kids pointed them out and the two big men rushed down to stop them. The officer continued to jabber down the phone and the two sets of twins were able to sneak past him and approach the bridge. When they arrived there, however, there were too many stewards and security people barring the way. One of them, a short, broad woman came over.

"What are you children doing here? There's an emergency going on. You should be in your cabins!"

"But we think we can help," said Minty.

"Don't be ridiculous. This situation is far too dangerous; now you need to go back." The woman waved her hands in a shooing motion.

Arvo stepped to the front. "But we know who is doing this – we know the crazy creature controlling the controls!"

"What? It's some kind of hairy... *thing!* How

can you possibly know that?"

"Well it's kind of long story," said Loogi, "with boy and cheese and sleepwalking and pills."

The woman took a deep breath and narrowed her eyes. "You lot are just wasting my time and getting in the way in the middle of a serious crisis – I've never heard such nonsense."

While this was going on, Ursule had climbed up onto one of the handrails outside the bridge. "Hey!" she shouted. "I can see him through the windows – a horrible shaggy creature jumping about inside. Prankenstein!"

At that moment, the cruise liner's emergency warning siren screeched into action again, deafening everyone gathered around the bridge. An automated voice boomed out:

"COLLISION WARNING! COLLISION WARNING!"

The four children ran back up onto the top deck again so they could see what was going on.

The volcanic island was now very near indeed and the ship had not slowed down at all. It was heading straight for a large sandy beach.

"Quick, everyone," cried Minty over the siren's

blare. "We're going to crash so find something really strong to hold onto."

The four of them grabbed the metal rail at the side of the deck and watched the island rear up, huge and menacing. Their hearts were racing as adrenaline surged through their bodies.

There was a deep, booming crunch and the ship bumped upwards, throwing all of the twins off their feet. Another one followed along with a horrible eerie noise like the sound of a dragon dying. The great cruise liner jarred and swayed as it ploughed into the sand of the shore, slowing suddenly as it rammed up the deserted beach and came to a grinding halt among palm trees.

As it finally stopped the four children slid forward, jolting together in a sore tangle of heads and knees and trainers. Groaning and aching they stood, rubbing their bruised limbs and checking that they were all OK. *The Queen of the Ocean* was no longer at sea.

22
Hello volcano

People all over the ship assessed their bruises and hobbled onto the outer walkways to see what had happened. Every single passenger was utterly astonished to see that their cruise liner was now planted on a white sandy beach on a small rocky island. Each person looked up and saw the great rumbling volcano above them, less than a kilometre away. It continued to puff out great plumes of black smoke. Not only could they see it and hear it but they could smell it.

"It's like burning tarmac," said Ursule. "Or that casserole you once made, Minty."

"Well, anyway, now we do what?" said Arvo.

"Wait for the rescue, I am hoping," said Loogi.

"We'd better go and check if our parents are all right. You'd better do the same for Soapy's parents," said Minty.

"Oh dear, I fear Mrs Thompson was just out of sick bay and now she's back in with the big head clonk," said Arvo.

"But what about Soapy? What about Prankenstein?" asked Ursule.

"What can we do? They won't believe us even if we tell them the truth," said Minty.

The four headed back to the cabins through crowds of tottering older people, many with fat lips and black eyes. Everyone looked dazed and lost.

"I'm not going to get orf and push," said one ancient lady.

They passed one of the security officers talking into his radio and confirming that the bridge was now back under the control of the Captain and that the hairy hijacker had escaped.

So Prankenstein's on the loose again, thought Arvo and Loogi at the same moment, sharing identical thoughts as twins sometimes do. *That's all we need.* It took some time in the chaos for the girls

to find their parents but they did eventually. To locate the Thompsons, the Twince followed the sound of Mrs Thompson's ranting voice which could be heard across half the ship.

"Are you all right, boys?" said Mr Thompson who saw them first. "What about Soapy? Isn't he with you?"

"Er, no, we are, er, not sure where he is," said Loogi.

Mrs Thompson's eyes were big and scary. "But you must know. Oh, we can't have lost our silly son again!"

"Where did you last see him?" said Mr Thompson.

Arvo gulped. "Well, er, well, we, er…"

Mrs Thompson glared into his eyes. "You two know something, don't you? What is it? Out with it!"

The Twince looked at each other but before Arvo could say another word there was a raucous metallic clank above their heads. Mr Thompson raced outside to see what it was and the boys followed. Mrs Thompson tried to call them back but they were only too glad to get away.

There on the deck above the cabin were large

fragments of black, steaming rock. The deck itself was dented.

"What happened?" said Mr Thompson to a nearby steward who was trying to guide people away as he choked and wiped grey smears off his face.

"It just came out of the sky – a dirty great hot rock. You really need to stay indoors, all of you."

The ship's intercom bing-bonged again telling everyone to return to their cabins but the Twince didn't fancy another interrogation from Soapy's mum. In the confusion caused by the smoke and passengers hurrying in all directions they stole off and headed for the games room.

"That was volcanic bomb," said Loogi as they hurried along the central corridor. "Even Prankenstein is not *that* dangerous."

There was no one in the games room and the Twince were surprised to discover that the ship's computers were still online. Loogi used a GPS app to locate their position and quickly discovered that the island they were on was called Rocher de la Mort.

He googled it and found that the volcano was called Mount Pulveriser.

"Erk, this is one of most active volcanoes in Indian Ocean," said Loogi. "Scientists believe it will erupt any day soon."

"Could it be now?"

Loogi did more searching. "Double erk. The island was evacuated two weeks ago, it says on BBC News. A large eruption last happened in 1972 and seismic readings indicate that an even larger one is due in the next three days."

"When was that news report?" said Arvo.

"Two days ago."

23
Prankenstein lost

In the games room the Twince sat and tried to think what to do. They were on a ship grounded on a tropical island next to a gigantic volcano that was about to erupt. Their best friend had turned into a prank-potty monster and had disappeared. His parents were now after them and no one on the ship would believe them. It didn't look good.

"Maybe we should just hide until rescue?" said Arvo.

"But how will we be rescued? This ship is marooned. It cannot move. There are thousands of people stuck on board."

"If the Captain is now back in control surely they have called 999 or whatever you do at sea. Maybe Royal Navy will arrive to help again?"

"But what about Soapy? What if Prankenstein is on the island? We have none of the idea where he is."

At that moment the boys held their breath as the games room door opened. It was Minty and Ursule.

"Hi boys," said Minty. "We thought we'd find you here. We told our parents we were just going to check you were OK."

"We have news," said Ursule. "Our dad asked one of the officers what happened on the bridge. He said that once the liner stopped on the beach the creature ran out of the bridge, grabbed a rope and swung down from the side of the ship. It was last seen scuttling into the jungle carrying part of a gangplank."

Before one of the Twince could respond there was another ringing boom above their heads, as if the vessel was being hit by a steam hammer.

"More volcanic bombs," said Loogi. "That volcano is going to do the blowing at any moment." He explained to the girls what the news report had said. His talk was interrupted by another intercom announcement.

"PLEASE LISTEN CAREFULLY. THE ROYAL NAVY HAS BEEN CONTACTED FOR ASSISTANCE AND THEY ARE SENDING

TWO SHIPS TO THE ISLAND TO RESCUE ALL PASSENGERS. FOR YOUR SAFETY IT IS ESSENTIAL TO STAY UNDER COVER TO AVOID BEING HIT BY ROCKS FROM THE ACTIVE VOLCANO. THE NAVY VESSELS ARE DUE TO ARRIVE WITHIN FOUR HOURS."

The four of them sat down and wondered about a plan.

"The trouble is that even if we tell them about Soapy and Prankenstein no one will believe us and so they won't go and look for him," said Minty.

"We will have to do it ourselves," said Arvo.

"But what about the volcano and flying lava bombs?"

"We must risk it," said Loogi. "We cannot abandon our friend."

"But how can we leave the ship? I don't think I can do a Tarzan exit like Prankenstein," said Ursule.

"And Prankenstein could be anywhere on the island," added Minty. "How will we find him?"

"Ah," said Loogi. "We can get him to come to us. We have something under our bed in the cabin, remember... cheese!"

They sat for another fifteen minutes, trying to figure out how to get off the huge ship when another announcement interrupted their thoughts.

"WOULD ALL PASSENGERS AND CREW PLEASE BE ON THE LOOKOUT FOR FIVE CHILDREN WHO HAVE BEEN REPORTED MISSING..."

The voice then gave their names and a description of each of them.

"Yikes, now we are the fugitives," said Arvo. "Everyone will be looking for us."

Minty opened the door of the games room and peered outside. A waft of grey smoke and ash floated into the room, causing everyone to cough. Minty yanked one of the small curtains off a porthole and tied it over her mouth, cowboy-style.

The others did the same.

"Now we *really* are the outlaws," said Loogi with a chuckle.

"The wind must have changed direction," said Ursule. "Hey, that means we should have cover to sneak out of here and maybe get off the ship."

The four of them tentatively stepped out of the room and into a haze of grey. The volcanic plume of smoke and ash was now drifting over the ship and cloaking it in an impenetrable fog.

Outside they could hear ominous deep rumbles and dark booms as more pressure built up inside the mountain.

The children shielded their eyes as well as they could then started to make their way along the side of the ship. It was only possible to see a few metres ahead but at least no one would spot them.

"Where are we going?" said Minty.

"I don't know, I was following you," said Arvo.

"Hey, look!" Ursule had stopped by a lifeboat. "There are instructions on how to operate this."

"A lifeboat? But we are on land now, not water," laughed Arvo.

"She is right, noodle brother," said Loogi between coughs. "The boat has crane for lowering us down onto sand. No one will see with this smoke."

"And they won't even hear us with the volcano making such a racket," said Minty. "Sis, you're a genius. Let's get it going!"

The four of them read the instructions and then pulled away the plastic cover to reveal the emergency button that switched on power to the winch that would allow the small yellow boat to be lowered down the side of the ship.

"Shall I press it?" said Minty? Before anyone could answer, a volcanic bomb the size of a motorbike whistled a few metres past Loogi's head and thudded into the sand on the beach below. Once more they smelt the overpowering waft of burning and sulphur.

"Press it," called Arvo. Minty pushed it before telling the other three to climb into the lifeboat. A motor inside the control box whirred into life and several lights on the panel lit up. Minty moved the main operating lever to the right and saw the thick metal cables on the crane arms above the boat begin to move. Wheels started turning and the yellow boat jolted as it was released from its coupling. It started to descend.

"Quick Minty, jump aboard," called Ursule, beckoning her twin through the suffocating grey ash which now coated everything in sight. Minty ran towards the boat and leaped over the low barrier at the ship's edge. She landed with a

thump on top of Arvo.

"Ooh, so sorry. Are you all right?"

"It was better than being socked by volcano bomb, I suppose," said Arvo, rubbing his elbows and nose.

The boat swayed as it dropped slowly down the side of the ocean liner. Above they could hear the gears of the winch grinding away. The beach below was not visible in the clouds of fiery fog around them.

"Well, this is certainly more interesting than a trip to the shops," said Ursule.

As they descended further they began to pass the portholes of the lower cabins. In one of them, Loogi saw the bewildered face of an elderly lady looking out, just a metre away. He smiled and waved.

"I think she may just have fainted," he said.

They passed another face at a window. This time Arvo smiled and waved. The face was slightly familiar, and strangely growly.

"Poop of the nincom! That was Soapy's mum!" cried Loogi. They all ducked down but it was too late.

"This is bad. Now they know what we're

doing," said Minty. "Worse too," said Ursule. "We forgot to pick up the cheese."

A moment later there was a sudden jolt which threw them all off their feet. The lifeboat had landed. Wafting the smoke out of their eyes the two pairs of twins climbed out onto the now speckled grey sand.

"Well, we made it," said Minty.

"How are we going to get back on board?" said Loogi.

No one had an answer to that question.

24
Jungle bungle

The jungle was dark, dirty and almost impossible to penetrate. The great cloud of ash from the volcano blocked out the light and made it difficult to see anything. The four children were hot and sticky and scared.

"We're not getting anywhere," said Minty. "This was a bad idea."

"Not a bad idea," said Arvo. "A terrible idea."

"Utterly trousers," added Loogi.

"You mean pants," said Ursule.

"We'll never find Prankenstein – he could be anywhere."

"And even if we do find him, he won't

come with us."

"He's probably got grisly pranks in store for us right now… jungly snakes…"

"Tigers…"

"Holes in the ground full of slime…"

"Or maybe he's going to use the volcano in some way – to perform the biggest prank in the history of existence…"

They plodded on for a few more minutes then stopped. They were thirsty, wheezing and lost. Arvo was about to ask which way the ship was when the ground beneath their feet began to shake. Loogi fell over and the trees around them were swaying and shivering. The shaking increased in magnitude and all four kids grabbed a branch to stop themselves being thrown to the ground.

"Is it an earthquake?" shouted Minty.

"Well, it's the only thing we haven't had on this trip so far," said Ursule.

For a moment the trembling stopped but only for a moment. When it started again it was even more violent and accompanied by an ear-splitting boom, an explosion that hit them like a donkey's kick, bashing their eardrums and knocking them

all down. After the great surge of pressure a hot wind ripped through the trees blowing away the cloud of ash and smoke.

Each of the four was stung in the eyes by particles of dust and flying debris. It felt like the end of the world, at the very least.

When the wind dropped, the air was suddenly clear. The ground was still trembling and there was a deep, grinding roar from above to accompany the rumbling. They all looked up and saw the volcano. Or rather, half a volcano because the top part appeared to be missing. In its place was a hissing churn of orange-red fire, spurting and spitting and bubbling. Out of the cone a blinding hot surge poured forth – a river of molten rock like an overspill of radioactive custard. It gushed from the broken mountain, racing down the slopes obliterating the jungle and everything in its path. It was coming their way.

They turned and saw the ship just three hundred metres down the beach. No one said a word. They just ran.

25
The big fry up

As the four charged up the beach they could
hear an angry crackling, hissing and crunching
behind them as the river of lava ate up the jungle
and surged towards the beach at the speed of a
galloping racehorse. They were all thinking the
same thing. *We can probably get to the ship but
will they see us? Will they be able to get us back
on board in time?*

As they neared the liner, Arvo spotted a
second lifeboat being lowered. Had they been
seen? Was it to rescue them? Or was it a search
party, alerted by Mrs Thompson? Either way,
it could surely be their lifeline.

Arvo tripped on a piece of slimy seaweed.
Loogi stopped to give him a hand up and Arvo saw
the horror in his brother's eyes as he looked back
along the sand. He turned and saw that the lava

had reached the far end of the beach and was now glooping towards them, white-hot and relentless.

The Twince looked back at the ship but the lifeboat had stopped descending. The crew had seen the molten rock flow and decided that they couldn't risk it. The children were stranded.

Minty and Ursule screamed and waved at the ship, still a hundred metres away, but it was no use. The lava was closing in fast. They weren't going to make it.

A different sound caught Arvo's ear and he turned round to face the sea. There, perhaps half a mile out a large grey-blue warship had appeared and a lot nearer was a small, noisy outboard inflatable boat, its engine screaming as it skidded over the waves and towards the children. On board were three figures wearing lifejackets.

"The Navy!" screamed Minty. "A rescue boat!"

The four children changed direction and sprinted towards the craft that bumped onto the beach. Two men leapt out and bellowed at the children to hurry. Loogi heard a great blast of hissing and looked over his shoulder. The first lava had crashed into the sea and a crackling, shattering blast of steam was the result. A big man grabbed

him under the armpit and whisked him towards the boat. Another carried Ursule through the lapping waves. Everyone was shouting and rushing. They could feel the lava's heat burning their faces.

All six tumbled into the small boat and the engine roared to life. All around, the lava crashed and bubbled and smashed its way onwards. The craft turned nimbly and skidded into deeper waters moments before the lava turned an evil black as it met the waves in a sizzle of fury at the point where they had just been rescued.

The men looked the children over and checked they were OK. One had an armband saying 'Medic'. He wiped his face and spoke.

"Close thing, kids. The ship radioed us to say you were on the island somewhere. As stupid ideas go, that must be one of the very stupidest."

"Yes, we're so sorry," said Minty. "But thank you for saving us."

Once the boat started to move away from the violence of the shore, the other man gave each of the children a lifejacket and the third crew member, a woman with a thick Scottish accent, cut the engine.

"Hang on a minute, we were told there were

five bairns. Where's the other one?"

"We are not knowing," said Loogi.

None of them wanted to try and explain about Prankenstein. Arvo was sure he would have found a way to escape the volcano anyway.

"What about the cruise ship?" said Ursule. "How will you rescue the passengers? Our parents are on board."

The two men looked at each other. "We really don't know, miss, sorry."

"But there must be something you can do," said Minty.

"There's not a lot you can do with a volcano like that."

Arvo had noticed that the sea had slowed down the lava by cooling it although the deadly orange flow was still approaching the ship.

"What will happen when the lava reaches the ship?" he asked.

The woman said, "You don't want to know, laddie."

"But I do want to know, that's why I am asking," replied a confused Arvo.

The sailors remained silent for a moment.

"The passengers will be all right, won't they?

The ship will protect them, surely," said Ursule.

The medic looked at her. "Yes, it'll protect them for a while."

"And then what?"

"Well, volcanic lava like this is about 1000 degrees. The ship is a big metal container. It's a bit like putting a saucepan over a gas flame."

"It's going to get very hot for them, isn't it?"

The woman nodded. "Aye, you could say that. It'll be more like the world's biggest fry up."

26
Surf's up

Minty was just deciding whether to cry over
the possibility of her parents being barbecued
on a beach when one of the men pointed towards
the navy ship which was about 400 metres away
from the small boat.

"What the heck's going on? The big guns
are moving." He grabbed a pair of binoculars
and started focusing while the children turned
to try and see what was happening. Sure enough
they could all make out one of the battleship's
enormous twin-barrelled guns swinging round
and lifting up so it was pointing towards the island.

The man's jaw fell as he got the binoculars
working.

"There appears to be... some kind of *ape* jumping
about on the deck by the guns. It can't be."

The other man grabbed the binoculars while

the woman radioed to the ship to ask what was going on.

The four children looked at each other and gulped: they knew what was going on.

Prankenstein.

The radio message back from the ship seemed to make no sense at all and the woman reported that all she could hear was shouting and running and people talking about jellyfish.

Minty watched in horror as the gun stopped. Its target was unmistakably the island. "He's not going to shoot *The Queen of the Ocean* is he? That surely is a prank too far."

Before anyone could answer there was a deep boom and a screaming whistle as something large and dangerous flew over their heads with incredible speed. The cruise ship, however, did not explode. Instead there was a blast of rocks and dust on the side of the erupting volcano near the top of the broken cone. The big gun fired again, striking in the same place. The Scottish woman screamed into the radio while trying to get the engine going.

The two men argued about what to do.

The third shot hit the mountain again but this time the effect was dramatic. A great slab of rock from the top lip of the volcano, the size of a large office block, began to crumble and fall. With a deep splintering reverberation, it leant inwards and fell into the churning spout of the volcano. Everyone watched as it wedged in the crater with a mighty boom, plugging the angry peak.

"I don't believe it," said the medic.

"What a shot," said the other man.

The children stared at the volcano and wondered if Prankenstein had done something heroic for once, something truly marvellous and amazing. Had he stopped the lava? Had he saved two and a half thousand passengers from being ingredients in the world's biggest cooked meal?

"Hang on, I don't think it's going to work," said the Scottish woman.

Everyone watched with hardly a breath: on the cruise liner, on the navy ship and on the little boat bobbing at sea. There were gaps in the big rock stopper at the top of the volcano and spurts of scorching lava were spraying out under enormous pressure hundreds of metres into the sky like perpetual fireworks.

On the liner the passengers felt the ship shudder as the ground once more began to shake. Loogi noticed a mosaic of ripples on the surface of the water. Steam and smoke and ash and volcanic bombs began to shoot out of cracks at the top of the now rumbling cone.

"The pressure is building," said Loogi.

"I think you're right, she's gonna blow," said the medic.

Before anyone else could speak there was another earth-ripping boom and once more everyone's eardrums were punched by a sonic wave of brutal intensity. The volcano gave a mighty molten sneeze and into the air shot the office-block chunk of mountain, like a meteor heading in the wrong direction. It went up and up, powered by a blast of unimaginably hot liquid rock which sprayed up and out and then gushed down the slopes again, once more heading for the

stranded ship on the beach.

"Mum! Dad!" cried Ursule.

But the giant plug of rock's ascent was not finished. It reached about 3,000 metres and then slowed and stopped for a fraction of a second in the sky before surrendering to gravity's eternal wish and plummeting back to earth with frightening speed. It rolled and crumbled as it fell, shards of granite, spitting out in its wake. The Twince wondered where it would land. Not on the ship, surely? Was *that* Prankenstein's final horrific prank?

The rock landed in the sea some distance away. There was a titanic splash and thunderous crunch as it hit the seabed and then the four children and three adults, still holding their breath, saw a big dark shape emerge from the water.

"Oh crivens, it's a wave the size of Ben Nevis," said the woman, grabbing at the engine controls.

Ursule thought to herself, *No, I was wrong*

*about the earthquake – there was one more disaster
to come…*

"We'll never outrun it," shouted the second
man. "We need to head into it and ride it."

"That's what I'm doing," said the woman. "We
might have to jump it."

Arvo, Loogi and the girls grabbed the ropes at
the edges of the boat and glanced at each other
again, gulping simultaneously.

The tsunami approached with astonishing
speed. The Scots pilot charged at it, the little
boat's engine screaming and before anyone knew
it they were sailing through the air. They landed
with a wet splat. They had survived.

"Look!" called Minty, pointing towards the island.
They watched as the giant wave smashed onto
the beach hitting the red-hot lava with a blinding
explosion of hissing steam. It also hit the ship and
an amazing thing happened. The big cruise liner
jolted one way and then the other before lifting
and sliding down the beach back into the ocean.

"The wave has rescued the ship!" cried Ursule,
clapping her hands, grinning and bursting into
tears at the same time.

Loogi put a hand on his brother's shoulder.

"Prankenstein has saved the ship again. First from the pirates and now from the tsunami. Perhaps he's not all bad, after all."

The medic was kneeling in the boat shaking his head. "Now I think I have seen everything."

The pilot cleared her throat and pointed back out to sea. "Not everything. Look."

It took the children a moment to work out what it was: a dark, squat figure standing legs apart and arms out on some kind of long, square board on top of a wave. They could all hear its voice hollering and whooping and squawking.

Prankenstein was surfing the tsunami.

He raced behind the island and disappeared.

27
Where is Soapy?

It was early evening by the time that the four children were back on board the cruise liner, which was now once more in the Indian Ocean, steaming away from the fiery island. Minty and Ursule were reunited with their relieved parents and poor Arvo and Loogi were returned to the situation they were now dreading: an interrogation by Mrs Thompson as to Soapy's whereabouts. First, however, they were checked over in the sick bay by the ship's doctor, then allowed to have a bath to clean off the layers of volcanic grime that had coated their skin.

"So, what do we say?" said Arvo as he pulled on some deliciously clean socks.

"Well, we tried to tell the truth before and they didn't believe us…"

"So we just say we don't know where Soapy is?"

Loogi nodded. "Correct. That is why we went

on island to search for him. It is also true."

"But Mrs Thompson still does not have her son back..."

"And even if he returns, there is still cheese on board."

When a nurse came to take them back to their cabin Arvo put up a hand. "Please, Mrs, Miss or Ms, I would like to have word with Captain."

"The Captain?" She raised her eyebrows considerably. "Why is that?"

"We need to get all Navy sailors on board to search this ship for cheese."

She rubbed his hair. "Well, the doctor said he couldn't find any severe bumps on your head but there must have been one. Your imagination is obviously completely scrambled. Forget all that – what you two need is a good night's rest."

The Twince walked as slowly as they could back to their cabin, past rows of staring and whispering passengers who now knew exactly who they were. The kindly nurse kept everyone back and then turned the last corner into their corridor.

There was Mrs Thompson, arms folded, lips twisted, waiting to pounce. Mr Thompson was trying to hold her back.

"Ah, good, I need a word with these two – *lots* of words," she growled.

She stepped forward menacingly but the nurse blocked her way.

"I'm sorry, Mrs Thompson but it'll have to wait until morning. The doctor has advised that these two need a full, undisturbed night's sleep. They've been through the ship crashing, a volcanic eruption, an earthquake and a tsunami in the last few hours."

"That's nothing compared to what I'm going to

do to them," she hissed.

"Please, they've had enough trauma for now. A security officer will be posted here all night." With that the nurse opened their cabin door and the twins scuttled inside with eyes down, their relief colossal.

The nurse made sure they were tucked up in bed then turned the lights down.

"Right, you two: no pranks, no escapes, no cheese tales, no nothing but sleep, all right?"

They both nodded. They were utterly exhausted.

The pair quickly drifted off to sleep thinking about returning home. *If only Soapy were safe as well…*

When morning did arrive the Twince woke up late. They yawned and stretched and remembered what had happened the previous day. It couldn't be true could it?

Outside the cabin the security guard was there and he said that no, nothing unusual had happened in the night and it had been so quiet he'd even dropped off for a little snooze at one point.

The boys got dressed quickly and wondered if they could sneak away to breakfast without being grabbed by Mrs Thompson. They might even be able to see Minty and Ursule. They crept up the corridor past the Thompsons' door and past Soapy's door.

"Hang on," said Loogi. "Should we check?"

"No... well, OK."

Arvo turned the handle and slowly pushed the door open. There in his bed, sleeping like a baby, was Soapy Thompson.

28
What happened?

Arvo whispered as loudly as he dared, shaking his friend by the shoulder. "Soapy, wake up!"

Soapy turned over and made a few noises.

Loogi prodded him gently on the nose. "Shine and rise, troublemaker."

Soapy gave a broad yawn, pulled himself up onto his elbows and rubbed both eyes.

"Where are we?" he croaked.

"I tell you where we are: lucky to be alive," said Arvo.

Soapy blinked as he sat up properly. "Eh? What you talking about?"

"Volcanoes? Tsunamis?"

Soapy shook his head. "You what?"

Loogi drew closer and looked him in the eye. "Wait. Soapy, do you have the headache?"

"No, I'm fine... Prankenstein can't have been

at work if that's what you're thinking."

The Twince looked at each other, completely speechless, while Soapy pulled himself out of bed and started asking about breakfast.

"Hold on, Soapy Thompson," said Arvo, lifting his palm. "Are you telling us, that you do not recall anything about an island, volcano or a Navy boat or jungle?"

He shrugged and shook his head. "Should I have done? Was it a film we watched in the ship's cinema last night? It must have been rubbish – I can't recall it at all."

Loogi stood up. "What about lava or crashing a liner on a beach or shooting a mountain with a big gun or surfing a giant wave?"

Soapy laughed. "I have no idea what you two are talking about."

At that moment the door flew open and in charged Soapy's mum followed by his dad. Her hug was like a flying rugby tackle and sent Soapy crashing onto the bed.

"Oh you're safe, you're safe, you're safe," she said about 800 times.

Soapy tried to unlock her arms from his neck.

"Mum, I can't breathe, you're strangling me,"
he hissed.

"I don't care," she said, "As long as you're safe."

Mr Thompson sat on the bed, rubbed his son's
back and gave an enormous sigh. "What on earth
happened? How did you get back here?"

Soapy wriggled out of his mum's grasp and
took a long breath. "What is everyone on about?
I haven't been anywhere. Just in my bed."

There was a moment's silence.

Soapy's mum tried to smile. "Well, it must
have been the sleepwalking. You probably got lost
on the ship in a trance and bashed your head and
forgot what happened or something."

Not another useless head-banging theory,
thought Loogi.

Soapy's dad gave a genuine smile. "Well, it
doesn't matter. You're here now, you're OK and
there's not going to be any more sleepwalking."

For the first time Soapy appeared to register
a memory. "Oh yes, my pills," he said. "They, er,
went missing…"

His mum produced a plastic container. "Look!
We went to the ship's medical officer and he put
out an appeal and one of the passengers came

forward with these. They're the same tablets as yours. I'll make sure you have one every night until we are home."

The Twince gave a silent jiggle of joy. *No more pranks, no more worrying about cheese, no more disasters!*

Soapy had a shower and then a hearty breakfast. He was desperate to know more about volcanoes and tsunamis from the Twince but his parents would not leave his side. That would have to wait. As he sat there he felt a light tickle at the top of his throat. Soapy twitched his nose and reached for a tissue. Before it reached his nostrils he let out a ripping sneeze. There followed a dull thud inside the front of his head followed by another and another. It was like his brain was being squeezed by a snake. *Oh dear.*

"Can we go out onto the upper deck?" he said to his mum. "I feel like some fresh air."

Soapy's mum agreed and the three Thompsons climbed the steps followed by Arvo and Loogi who hadn't yet noticed the headache. When they reached the top viewing deck they saw Minty, Ursule and their parents along with a small crowd gathered there.

They were pointing upwards and chattering briskly.

The girls saw Soapy and gave a small squeak of surprise, waving furiously but also realising they shouldn't draw too much attention to him. Minty made a strange face at the Twince and pointed up, half giggling. The Thompsons walked over to where they could see what everyone was staring at.

There above the bridge was the ship's tall white communications tower. On top of it was the revolving radar antenna, a large metal bar turning steadily. Today, however, it was different. There were two ropes hanging from its ends and on the bottom of each rope was a wriggling, squealing person, flying around as if on an extra-dangerous

fairground ride. One was Mr Pew and the other was Mrs Pew.

"Spewy!" said Soapy, suddenly feeling better.

His dad nodded. "It certainly is spewy – I think they're being sick right now – stand back."

Arvo smiled as they retreated to a safe distance. "What they need are barf bags."

Within a few minutes the antenna was shut down and the two dangling pukey passengers were rescued by stewards using ladders.

Ah, there's always one last prank, thought Soapy. *And Prankenstein, that was a beauty.*

Two burly security officers were called via the intercom to interview the Pews about what happened and Loogi surprised everyone by stepping forward and speaking to one of them as he strode to the scene of the strange incident. The conversation was brief.

"What did you say?" Arvo asked his brother as he returned.

"I told them I am thinking they should check the Pews' mobile phone call history."

Soapy leaned over to join the whispered conversation. "But why?"

Before Loogi could answer, Mrs Thompson ushered them all away saying that she was getting cold out here and needed a cup of strong coffee.

They sat for a whole, frustrating hour in the ship's Italian café with the Thompsons who were once again arguing with each other about who could have possibly tied up the Pews and why. The boys found it impossible to talk and wondered how they could get away. Soapy was just about to ask if he could have another drink when the door opened and a big white-uniformed man strode over to their table. It was the security officer that Loogi had spoken to up on the viewing deck.

"Er, could I have a word please?" he said to the Thompsons.

Mrs Thompson's face fell. "Oh no, please, not more trouble?"

"Well, no, not really – I'm here to congratulate these boys."

Soapy's mum nearly choked on a biscuit. "Really? Are you *sure*?"

"Yes, this young man gave us a tip-off and it has proved to be extremely valuable." He extended a finger towards Loogi who half-smiled.

"What do you mean, a 'tip-off?'" said Mr Thompson.

"Well, we checked Mr and Mrs Pew's mobile phone call history as the smart boy here suggested and we discovered some very interesting things. There were a number of calls and texts to the same number, based on the mainland."

"What? Eh? I don't get it," said Soapy.

Loogi ignored him. "Let me guess: was it belonging to, by any chance, one of those pirate henchymen who hijacked the ship?"

"That's right," said the security man. "The Pews were giving them information – leading them to the ship."

Mrs Thompson shook her head in amazement. "You mean to say, that Mr Pew and his wife helped those horrid armed criminals to hijack this ship?"

"Exactly."

"But why?"

Loogi put up a finger. "I am guessing for a cut of the money they were supposed to grab off the passengers."

The security man smiled. "Right again! We passed on the information to police and they discovered that this couple have done this nine times before, with other pirate teams too. The authorities are now rounding all of them up thanks to the information you led us to. You boys have solved a crime that's been baffling the

Navy and cruise companies for years."

Mrs Thompson just sat and stared but Mr Thompson gave Loogi a huge pat on the head and called, "Well done, Loogs!"

Arvo and Soapy patted him on the back and laughed.

"How did you know?" said Soapy.

Loogi gave a little shrug. "I am using my puzzle-solving skills and noticing things. A bit of the deduction, a bit of the observation, a bit of the research... And I overheard them talking about it in the toilets."

Everyone laughed this time.

"Well," said the man. "The Captain has heard about this and he would like to give you three lads a small reward. How would you like to come up onto the bridge of the ship?"

29
Best to keep your mouth shut

The main control room of *The Queen of the Ocean,* the bridge, was much larger than the boys expected. When Arvo, Loogi and Soapy arrived, they were ushered in and the senior officers in their gold-braided uniforms gave the trio a hearty round of applause.

"Our heroes," said the captain. "Welcome to the bridge of our 128,000 ton ocean liner."

The three walked forward sheepishly.

This has worked out quite well, thought Arvo.

Better than being interrogated by Mrs Thompson, thought Loogi.

Forget Prankenstein the villain, I'm a hero now, thought Soapy.

They were introduced to the top commanders of the ship and shown some of the computers,

navigation systems and controls. There were hundreds of switches, tens of screens and huge banks of dials, flashing lights and buttons.

"OK, which one of you is Bogie?" said the Captain.

"I am Loogi," said Loogi.

"Yes, Lurgy, I hear that you did some splendid work tracking down those pirates. How would you like to take the wheel?"

"Where do I take it?" said Loogi.

"I think he means do the steering of the ship," said Arvo.

Loogi stepped forward and tentatively took hold of the small wooden ship's wheel, keeping it as steady as he could.

"Don't worry," said the captain. "The main computer won't allow you to do anything drastic unless you override it."

After this Arvo had a turn and was also nervous about being in control. He declined when the Captain asked if he'd like to change speed.

"What about the last young man, Soaky?" said the captain. "You don't look shy. I'm sure you'd like to speed us up a little."

Soapy stepped forwards eagerly. "Sure," he

said, grabbing the wheel.

The captain stepped beside him and was just about to explain what to do when Soapy leaned forward, punched three buttons on the power control unit, flicked a switch and then expertly slid the main propulsion lever forward. The dials immediately showed increased power to the engines and everyone noticed the ship begin to pick up speed, punching through the waves.

The captain stood and stared. "How on earth did you know how to do that?"

Soapy quickly pulled his hand back from the throttle lever. His mouth opened then closed again then opened just a fraction.

"Erm, I'm... not... really... sure."

Every senior officer stood, speechless.

Arvo looked at his watch. "Oh, look, we really must be going." Loogi nodded.

"Yes, it's so, er, late."

Soapy just ran.

Other books in the series